THREE'S A CROWD

CHRISTY MCKELLEN

B

Boldwood

First published in Great Britain in 2024 by Boldwood Books Ltd.

Copyright © Christy McKellen, 2024

Cover Design by Leah Jacobs-Gordon

Cover Photography: Leah Jacobs-Gordon

A CIP catalogue record for this book is available from the British Library.

Paperback ISBN 978-1-83617-077-8

Large Print ISBN 978-1-83617-076-1

Hardback ISBN 978-1-83617-075-4

Ebook ISBN 978-1-83617-078-5

Kindle ISBN 978-1-83617-079-2

Audio CD ISBN 978-1-83617-070-9

MP3 CD ISBN 978-1-83603-999-0

Digital audio download ISBN 978-1-83617-072-3

Boldwood Books Ltd
23 Bowerdean Street
London SW6 3TN
www.boldwoodbooks.com

To my darling Verto.
This one's for you, my brave, brave son.
I'm in awe.
Love you always.

1

SIX YEARS AGO

The day was perfect, yet also imperfect.

Trouble was on the way; Daisy Malone could feel it in her bones. Though exactly what sort of trouble was anyone's guess.

Looking around the table at the gathered guests, she experienced a shiver of apprehension, but told herself not to be ridiculous. Nothing could go wrong in such an idyllic setting with such a lovely group of people around her.

A banner bearing the words 'Happy Silver Wedding Anniversary' drifted languidly behind her in the cool breeze, where it hung between two cherry trees in the garden of the rented cottage. In the distance, brightly coloured dinghies bobbed in Fowey harbour and just below the cliff, where the cottage resided, waves gently lapped at the shore of a cove.

The waning, end-of-the-summer sun bathed the garden in golden light, highlighting the cheerful daisies that crowded the borders alongside the camomile lawn, their sweet fragrance mingling with the tang of salt in the air.

The guests of honour, Andy and Sally Carmichael, beamed at everyone gathered around the long, makeshift table, now laden with half-empty plates and the remainder of the feast their oldest friends, the Malones, had planned for them as part of their long weekend celebration. The table had groaned under the plates of cold meats, smoked salmon and delicate savoury tarts, surrounded by big bowls of colourful salads, couscous and thick wedges of soft granary bread.

They were all stuffed.

Daisy's father, Jack, raised his glass. 'A toast, to the best friends we could ever hope to have, and their wonderful boys.' He nodded to Adam and Sam, who had happily agreed to travel down to the coastal town in Cornwall to celebrate with them. 'May there be many more celebrations together to come. To Andy and Sally.' Everyone raised their glasses and a chorus of voices repeated, 'Andy and Sally.'

As an only child, it had always heartened Daisy to have the Carmichaels as her surrogate extended family.

They'd not gathered like this since the summer, two years ago, when she was sixteen, and it was wonderful to all be together again.

She'd missed them all.

Particularly the extra *someone* who hadn't made it to the party yet.

As if reading her thoughts, Sam, the baby of the family – though only a year younger than Daisy – asked, 'Where's Zach? I thought he was supposed to be getting in at six o'clock. It's almost nine now.'

Adam shrugged. 'You know Zach. He's a law unto himself.'

At the sound of his name, goosebumps broke across Daisy's skin.

Trouble personified.

Adam leant over and stole a couple of crisps that she'd left on her plate, giving her a sly wink.

She grinned back, glad of the distraction.

She'd always liked Adam. He was headstrong, but kind, with sky-blue eyes and a warm smile, all of which had the effect of charming the metaphorical pants off most girls he met. Daisy had always been vaguely aware that he was attractive, but she'd never felt anything romantically for him. He was too much like a brother for that.

'I miss holidays with you lot,' she said to him, offering him the bread that still sat forlornly on her plate.

He shook his head, patting his belly to display exactly how full he was.

'Yeah, we had a laugh, didn't we?' he said, leaning back in his chair and having a good stretch.

'Hey, do you remember—' she started to say.

'—burying Sam in the sand and running off and leaving him?' Adam finished for her, grin-grimacing at the memory.

'Yeah. So dangerous. He was terrified we weren't coming back, poor thing,' Daisy said, mirroring Adam's contrite expression. 'Thank God we didn't bury him that deeply and he managed to escape. We were real idiots back then.'

'I felt terrible about that – but then we got distracted because Zach went missing. Do you remember? We found him hours later in the dunes with his hand in that girl's bra,' Adam said with a proper grin this time.

Daisy remembered that well. And the sting of jealousy she'd felt at the sight of the girl draped all over Zach, lapping up his undivided attention. She'd hated the fact someone else had broken into their cosy foursome. It was meant to be just *them* hanging out together all summer. Like they always had.

'You projectile vomiting ice-cream all over the floor of that café... I have a vivid memory of that. Just the sight of a banana split still makes me queasy,' she said, trying to pull her thoughts away from Zach and the way he always managed to get her back up in some way or other.

'That shop keeper accusing you of stealing,' Sam chipped in from across the table where he'd abandoned his conversation with Daisy's dad about A level subjects.

'Oh yeah. He grabbed me and wouldn't let me go. I thought Zach was going to lamp him, he was so angry.' She felt hot and tingly at the memory of it. The look on Zach's face had stayed with her for a long time after that. He'd been ferociously protective of her, which had surprised her.

'Ah! Skinny dipping in the freezing cold sea,' Adam cut in, his smile wide.

She frowned. 'I don't remember that.'

Adam shrugged. 'I must be wishful thinking.' There was a strange look in his eyes now that made her a little uncomfortable. Was he *flirting* with her? *How weird.*

She changed the subject fast. 'Ugh, and Zach bought those soap sweets from the joke shop and handed them round to us like they were real ones. They were disgusting.'

Adam looked a little fazed by her sudden conversational curve-ball, but he seemed to pull himself together quickly.

'He got his dad with those back at home and got belted for it,' he said grimly.

'Seriously? I didn't know that.' Her stomach gave a strange flip, bringing with it a rush of nausea. Poor Zach. He may have been a troublemaker when he was young, but he definitely didn't deserve to be treated like that by his own father.

Adam had met Zach near the end of primary school, when the latter had joined after being excluded from his last place and ever since then, Zach had practically lived at the Carmichael's house. His mother had died when he was young and his father didn't pay him much attention, sometimes neglecting to buy food and instead using his money to fuel his alcoholism, which he'd suffered with since his wife had passed away.

Adam had let this all slip to her when they were fourteen, telling her that Zach would go home with him every day after school, so as not to be on his own in his house for hours. Sally, who had despaired at Zach's thin appearance and dirty clothes, would feed him and provide fresh ones, folding him into their family until he was considered as much a part of it as Adam and Sam.

'He's lucky he ended up with you as a best friend,' she said, giving Adam a conspiratorial smile.

'Yeah. He was out of control when I first met him. Loyal friend though. He got me out of a lot of scrapes.'

Her body gave an involuntary shiver. The way he'd made her feel whenever he was around had always had a strange vibe of danger to it. Not that she could put her finger on why. She knew he'd never physically hurt her or let anything bad happen to her. It wasn't in his nature.

'When did you last see him?' she asked tentatively. She didn't want to appear to be *too* interested in the ins and outs of Zach's life. She got the feeling Adam wouldn't be pleased to hear she had a weird love/hate thing about his best friend. Not that he'd said anything of the sort. But now she thought about it, there was something in Adam's manner towards her, ever since they'd arrived here, that made her suspect there was a little more to the way he felt about her than just brotherly love or plain friendship.

She wasn't quite sure how to feel about that.

'I met up with him in London about six months ago,' Adam replied, pushing his fingers through his short, blond hair and making his fringe stick up in messy peaks.

He was a pretty sexy guy, Adam, when she considered him properly. Good looking. And smart.

Stop it, Daisy. That's too weird to think about right now.

'It must be going on for two years since I've seen him... It'll be good to see him again,' she said, not able to look Adam in the eye now as she tried to divert her thoughts away from the unsettling direction they'd been heading.

Standing up, she clapped her hands together awkwardly, needing to move about. 'Right. Well, I'm going to go and chop some fruit for dessert,' she said, even though she was pretty damn sure no-one was going to be able to eat it, judging by all the food everyone had left on their plates.

But she needed to do something to quiet the nervous tension that was making her limbs twitchy.

'Um. Okay. Want a hand?' Adam asked.

'Nah. I'm good, thanks,' she said, already moving

away from the table. The introvert in her needed a few minutes on her own to recharge before Zach appeared. 'Back in a mo.'

She strode off towards the kitchen of the holiday house before anyone could say anything else. Something made her glance back at the table though and she saw with a start that Adam was watching her with a wistful look on his face, which he quickly changed to a smile.

Weirder and weirder.

Entering the cool of the kitchen, she leant against the work surface, making sure she was out of sight of the people in garden. She didn't want to be caught looking anything but composed by either Adam or Zach – when the latter finally deigned to turn up, that was.

Gathering the fruit and a chopping board, knife and a bowl, she thought back to the last time she'd seen him. They'd all come on holiday to Fowey for a week during the school holidays and, as usual, Zach had joined them.

He'd been strange with her for the whole week. Sort of withdrawn when she was around and even more sarcastic and eye-rolly than usual whenever she spoke. When Sally had found her having a cry about it in her bedroom after a particularly cutting remark Zach had made to her, she'd reassured her it was nothing to do with her. Boys Zach's age weren't great at relating to girls and often hid their confusion behind cruelty. She should just ignore him.

If only it was that simple, Daisy had thought at the time.

He was an integral part of her holidays and she missed the sibling-like camaraderie they all used to share when they were younger.

Just as she thought this, there was a shout of greeting from outside and, peering through the kitchen window into the garden, she saw a familiar tall, athletic figure marching across the lawn towards the table where the rest of the party sat.

Zach.

So, here he was. Finally.

Even from a distance, she could see he still radiated the same inexplicable appeal she'd always been bamboozled by.

'Hey, you made it!' she heard Adam say, getting up from his chair to meet his friend half way to the table and clap him on the back.

Zach was turned away from her, but she could make out the deep, bass tone of his voice as it floated on the breeze towards the open kitchen door. 'Yeah.

Bloody British trains. Mine was cancelled and the next one was late and my phone ran out of juice.'

Sam got up from where he was sitting on the other side of the table, bringing his food with him – how could he still be eating? Daisy, wondered – and walked over to give Zach a rough-looking, one-armed bear hug. 'Dude. Glad you made it. We thought you might not be coming.'

'Wouldn't miss it for the world, Sammo.'

Daisy continued to watch him surreptitiously out of the window as she added some chopped banana to the fruit salad. He was chatting amiably to Sam now. Even after all this time, she was still bothered by the same mingle of apprehension and excitement when she looked at him. At one time, they'd all been at sixes and sevens, one minute enjoying each other's company and the next, fighting like cats and dogs, but Zach seemed much surer of himself now. More adult. He held himself proudly and his face radiated confidence.

Drama school had been good for him.

'Hey, Zach, you eaten? Sorry we didn't wait. We were all starving,' Sam said.

'No worries. This'll do me,' Zach replied, grabbing a lonely looking sandwich from the plate Sam was holding.

Sally came bustling over and enveloped him in a motherly hug.

'Zach! You're here. We nearly gave up on you.'

'Sorry, Sally.' He returned her hug then turned to address the rest of the gathering still sitting at the table. 'Gordon. Alright Andy. Hi Lizzy.'

'So? How's it going? It's been ages,' Adam asked, motioning to follow him to the table and pulling out the chair next to him so Zach could sit in it.

'Yeah, fine. Come to London again soon. I miss having you around. The place is full of wankers.'

'Yeah, I heard that. Thought you'd fit right in,' Adam replied, shooting his friend a teasing grin.

Jealousy jabbed at her. She didn't imagine she'd be invited along to that get-together. Not that she should care. Zach would probably only tease or maybe ignore her the whole time anyway, based on her last experience of being around him, which wouldn't be a lot of fun. She dumped the last bit of fruit into the bowl, took a breath and readied herself to take it outside.

'We'll hit the bars, get trashed, nearly get arrested... It'll be like old times,' Zach was saying, his voice laden with mirth.

Stepping up to the open doorway, she saw his

mouth curving into a wide smile and her heart did a weird judder in her chest.

She took another moment to study him from a distance, while she could. His dark eyes, framed by long lashes, gave him that brooding look she remembered so well from years past and his jet-black hair, which was currently longer than he used to wear it, the fringe pushed away from his face, made him look older than she knew he was. He wasn't a pretty boy type, like Adam. His features were too angular for that, a little too harsh. But he wasn't without his own particular type of beauty. It was wilder, more nebulous and difficult to describe. She supposed some people might call it sex appeal. He certainly gave the impression he was a very sexual being from the way he moved... and brooded. Like he was always thinking wayward thoughts.

The idea shot a frisson up her spine.

Zach glanced around the garden. 'Is Daisy here?' he asked, as if she might be hiding in among her namesake flowers.

That was her cue. Exiting the kitchen, she made her way towards the table with the dessert, a pulse beating hard in her throat.

It took him a few moments to notice her walking towards them, but when he did, he seemed to stop what he was saying to Adam in mid-sentence and stared at her in what appeared to be shocked confusion.

The last time they'd been together, she realised, she'd been a slightly goofy looking beanpole of a girl. Not the woman she was now. Since then, her figure had not just blossomed, but bloomed and she'd finally grown into her once overly large features: wide-set eyes, Roman nose and full mouth.

The penetrating frown he was now giving her made her tremble, causing the slightly wet glass bowl she was holding to slip out of her hands. It shattered on the stone flags and everyone else turned to look at her. She stared down, aghast, at the mess of fruit and glass: a tutti-frutti at her feet.

As one, they all got up from the table and hurried over to help clear up the mess, laughing good naturedly at her embarrassment. Sam patted her on the back in a consoling manner before heading into the kitchen to grab a bin liner to put the destroyed dessert into.

Daisy was *mortified*.

She couldn't bring herself to even glance at Zach and see the look of exasperated amusement she felt sure must be written all over his face.

'Still as clumsy as ever, Daisy,' Adam teased, carefully collecting big chunks of glass with his hands.

Daisy smiled weakly at him.

Frustratingly, in the last year or so, she'd begun to feel much more comfortable in herself – finally starting to grow into the person she wanted to be as an adult. Until Zach had turned up and wrecked her peace of mind. Now, under his scrutinising gaze, she felt like the gangly, chaotic schoolgirl she used to be again.

Her mum came over to give her a sympathetic hug. 'Don't worry, I don't think any of us had room for pudding,' she murmured. 'Anyway, it looks like the rain is on its way now, so it's probably time to go inside.'

The day had started out sunny and warm, but now Daisy glanced up, she saw dark clouds had started to build in the sky. As the sun was well on its way to setting, the air had become cool and damp and she imagined she could taste the oncoming rain.

'Yeah, let's clear this table up and go inside,' suggested Andy, getting to his feet from where he'd been kneeling picking up grapes and bits of apple. They all murmured in agreement.

'Hey, look, why don't you kids get off to the pub so we adults can get drunk here in peace. We'll clear the rest of the table,' Sally said, waving the four of them away.

'Okay. We'll take everything inside, then we'll get out of your hair and leave you to your debauchery,' Zach said with a wink, grabbing a water carafe and a butter dish from the table and heading indoors.

They all voiced their amused agreement at that suggestion.

Daisy grabbed a pile of plates and – carefully – carried them in through the kitchen door. Just as she stepped inside, a gust of wind blew her hair across her face, obscuring her vision and she bumped into a large, hard body coming back out of the doorway.

She gave a little yelp, desperately gripping the pile of plates so as not to smash those as well.

Blowing her hair out of her eyes, she looked up into Zach's – familiar, yet somehow not – face and sucked in a ragged breath. His intense gaze bored into hers and, strangely, his expression seemed to mirror the look of bewilderment she knew had to be written across her own face.

'Watch where you're going there, Dizzy,' Zach said, snapping them out of the strange moment. He held up both hands, taking a dramatic step back-wards as if it was entirely possible for her to knock his six-foot, broad-chested body out of the way with her five-foot-nothing, dinky one.

The sound of her childhood pet name brought her up short. No-one had called her that in a long time. She'd made it perfectly clear that she hated it, so everyone had respected her wishes and stopped using it.

Except Zach.

Her hackles rose.

He hadn't changed at all.

'Nobody calls me that any more. And why don't *you* watch it, idiot,' she said, shooting him a disgruntled frown.

He flashed her a wolfish grin back.

'Still the same old Diz,' he murmured.

Before she could reply, he raised his hand and tucked a rogue bit of hair, that was still hanging over her face, behind her ear, bringing with him his *oh* so familiar scent that made her think of all their childhood holidays together. It sent a shock of such intense nostalgia through her body, her breath got trapped in her chest, making her feel slightly dizzy.

Huh. Maybe he was on the money with her nickname suiting her after all.

'Oh, sod off!' she muttered, frustrated by her response to him. How old was she? It was like she'd regressed to being thirteen again.

She pushed past him, not caring that she stepped on his foot, and headed into the kitchen where she dumped the pile of plates onto the work surface with a loud clatter.

The sound of deep, male laughter drifted in through the open door and Daisy dropped her head into her hands in frustration.

How did she always manage to make a fool of herself in front of him?

How?

Normally, she was a confident person, in control of her emotions and actions, but she seemed to have turned into a gibbering wreck in the face of Zach's *bloody annoying* presence.

So much for looking forward to seeing him.

She sighed and started to stack the plates into the dishwasher, giving the surge of adrenaline rushing through her veins an outlet.

This weekend was turning out to be even more of a trial than she'd anticipated.

2

Leaving the adults to clean up the kitchen, Adam, Sam, Zach and Daisy strolled down through the steep, narrow streets that led into the centre of Fowey. Colourful terraces lined the way, many sporting bright window boxes housing festoons of delicate trailing flowers. Further down, they passed independent clothes and knick-knack shops, their eclectic displays drawing them in for a closer look.

'So, which pub are we going to?' Adam asked, looking around at them all with raised eyebrows.

'The Ship Inn?' Zach suggested.

'Is that the one we got kicked out of a couple of years ago, when Adam puked all over the doorstep?'

They all guffawed.

'Do you think they'll remember us?' Daisy asked.

'Nah,' said Adam, batting away her question. 'Hope not anyway, I'm gasping.'

When they finally reached the Ship Inn, a quaint little pub overlooking the harbour, they found it thronged with people.

'Look, someone's just leaving that table in the corner. Let's grab it,' Adam said, already making a bee-line for it.

They squeezed around it, Daisy jammed in between Adam and Sam. There were only three chairs though so Zach, as the last one to make it over, was left standing.

'I'll get the drinks in then,' Zach said, deadpan.

Adam grinned, as if his cunning ploy had worked. 'Great. Lager all round?'

'I'll have a rum and coke,' Daisy said.

Zach turned to give her an incredulous look, then, when she held her ground and stared him down, gave a curt not and walked off towards the bar. Daisy noticed a group of women at a nearby table watch him pass them, giggling, then whispering to each other. He ignored them, but Daisy could swear he pulled himself up taller and deepened his swagger.

'So, Daisy. I guess you're off to uni really soon?'

Adam said into her ear, making her jump and drag her gaze away from Zach's retreating figure.

'Hmm? Er, yeah. Off to Manchester in a couple of weeks. I can't wait. I'm sick of being at home. My mum's driving me nuts, flapping around and staring at me tearfully when she thinks I'm not looking.'

'Empty nest syndrome. Our mum was the same when I first left.'

'Yeah. I feel a bit bad about leaving them, but it's time.'

'You're going to love uni. I think I'm going to actually have to do some work this year though. Maybe go out every other night, cut back a bit, you know?' he said with a smile.

'Hmm.' Daisy was distracted by the sight of Zach returning to the table with a tray loaded with their drinks. Somehow, he'd managed to get served straight away, even though there was a crowd three people deep at the bar.

He nodded curtly to her as he reverently placed her rum and coke in front of her.

'Milady.'

'Thanks.' She gave him a friendly smile, determined not to hold his previous slight towards her against him.

She'd just be really cool about it. Like a grown up.

Zach handed Sam and Adam their drinks, then took his own and leant against the wall next to where Sam was sitting as there still wasn't a free chair for him.

Daisy was so squashed in between Adam and Sam, she had trouble raising her glass to her lips.

Taking a sip, she looked up to see Zach was studying her with a puzzled look in his eyes. Was he wondering where the old tomboy Daisy had gone?

'So, Zach. How's drama school?' Sam said, making Zach turn away from her to look at him. 'You know, if you'd asked me when we were younger if you'd end up as an actor, I'd have said no way.'

'Yeah, I know. I just kind of fell into it at school when I was bored one lunchtime and the drama teacher asked me to stand in for one of the kids in the play she was putting on. The idea of pretending to be someone else – getting right into their psyche – appealed to me. And I love the camaraderie of being part of a group all working towards the same goal. The after parties are pretty fucking cool too.' He flashed them all his wolfish grin.

'Isn't it a bit pricey?' Sam asked.

'What, drama school? Nah. Not really. I got in on a scholarship.'

Sam nodded, his mouth lifting at one corner in approval. 'What does your old man think about it?'

Zach shrugged. 'Don't know. I haven't spoken to him in two years. He was barely ever sober enough to hold a conversation with anyway.'

The previous warmth of the atmosphere seemed to plummet and they all shifted uncomfortably in their seats.

'I bet you're getting plenty of action from all those gorgeous actresses though?' Sam said, in a clear, but somewhat naïve, attempt to lighted the tone.

'It's just "actors" for both sexes. And I can't complain. There're always plenty hanging around.' He folded his arms and gave a nonchalant shrug. 'You know what women are like: love me, need me, screw me, heal me,' Zach said, for some reason choosing to address this towards Daisy.

She shot him a hard glare back, one eyebrow raised in disdain.

'Sorry Daisy, I forgot there was a girl present,' Zach said, with a grin, clearly not sorry at all.

Anger burned in her chest, but she also experienced a sinking feeling of disappointment. Clearly, he still didn't think of her as a grown woman. Choosing not to rise to it, she just rolled her eyes at him, then stared down into her drink so he wouldn't notice how hot her cheeks were.

She was horrified by the thought of all those women willing to fall into bed with him as soon as he snapped his fingers; it sickened her. Couldn't they sense how little they meant to him?

She sat in silence for a while, feeling churned up and studiously ignoring him as the rest of them chatted. Why was she suddenly so uncomfortable here with them all? What had happened to their tight-knit gang of four from only a few years ago? It made her want to weep.

'I'm off to the gents,' Zach said suddenly, pushing away from the wall and dumping his half-drunk pint onto the table.

Daisy didn't watch him go this time.

'Yeah. Me too,' Sam said, sliding out from behind the table to leave Adam and Daisy on their own.

'You know I can't believe how different you look since the last time I saw you,' Adam said as soon as they'd gone, apparently not having noticed the tension growing between her and Zach. 'You used to be so... I don't know... boysy... when you were young. I used to think of you as one of us.' He held up his hands. 'Not that you haven't always been attractive. No offence meant.'

She smiled, despite herself. 'None taken. I was never very interested in make-up and hair and looking feminine, but I guess I changed as I grew up?' She twitched one shoulder and grinned. At least someone had noticed she wasn't the same girl she used to be.

'Your hair really suits you long too. And I love the short fringe. Very French chic,' he said, with a slow nod of approval.

'Thanks,' she said, moving her hand to self-consciously tug on a curl at the end of her hair. The same curl Zach had tucked behind her ear earlier.

'I can hardly believe you're the same girl I used to go skinny dipping with,' Adam said, his eyes twinkling with humour.

Daisy couldn't help but grin back. 'You know, I think you're getting me mixed up with some other boysy girl from your past.'

There was a loud snorting sound and Daisy turned to see Zach had returned to the table and was sitting down in Sam's place.

'Sorry, Zach, what was that?' Adam said, sounding miffed at the rude interruption.

Daisy jumped, but forced herself not to jerk away, as Zach's leg pressed against hers.

Heat rushed across her skin where their limbs touched, from thigh to knee.

'Nothing. Just got something caught in my throat,' Zach said, in the lazy drawl he always employed when he was in teasing mode. 'Massive queue for the gents so I'll go later.'

Sam came back too then and started asking Zach some more about drama school, so Daisy was relieved when Adam re-engaged her in conversation about her upcoming start at university, giving her tips on what to expect and what to avoid.

She'd forgotten how sweet Adam could be. He still had the same boyish looks as when he was young, but now with an added strong jaw line and sculpted cheekbones. He was tall too, although not as tall as Zach, who seemed to tower over her. Adam seemed really interested in what she had to say about why she'd chosen to do a media degree and she began to relax in his comfortable company, sipping her drink until it was gone.

Sam went and fetched them more drinks from the bar with Adam's ID and soon she'd drunk that too. She was feeling slightly woozy now, but she was enjoying Adam's company and found herself touching his arm when making a point about something. She was telling him about her plans for getting some work experience at a radio station during the holidays from uni when she became aware that she was being watched. Turning her head, she locked gazes with Zach, who frowned back at her, his dark eyes narrowed. There was something else in his expression too, but she couldn't quite discern what it was.

They were so close like this, their faces only centimetres apart.

His familiar scent hit her senses and she breathed him in, her head swimming with the intensity of their intimacy.

Out of nowhere, an unaccustomed throb began to beat, deep in the centre of her, as if he'd gently dragged his fingers up the flesh of her thighs. Her whole body tingled at the thought and she squirmed under his gaze.

'What?' she asked, not sure what to do with this strange new feeling. Especially not here in the pub.

'Nothing,' he murmured, 'just listening,' before turning away and talking to Sam again.

Daisy let out a sigh and rolled her eyes at Adam, who smiled benignly back at her.

'Actors,' he faux-whispered. 'Always creeping people out by studying them for future roles.'

Daisy laughed, which mercifully broke the tension.

* * *

After they'd all finished a third drink, they weaved back up to the cottage, in good spirits now, Sam chattering away, barely taking a breath to allow anyone else to get a word in. Luckily, the rain had held off and the night had turned balmy.

Daisy was conscious that Zach didn't once directly address or even look at her again and even though Adam and Sam were sandwiched between them, she was still acutely aware of his brooding presence, just feet away from her. What was his *problem*?

He'd always treated her with an offhand sort of disdain, sure, which she'd assumed was because she was a girl, younger than him, and akin to being a kid sister. But now? When they were all practically adults. Why could he still not bring himself to be civil towards her?

As they approached the house, Adam fell back slightly and caught Daisy by the hand. 'Can I talk to you on your own for a sec?' he asked, his expression startlingly serious.

She wondered what it could be – nothing *too* serious, she hoped – but decided to go with it. Nerves thrumming, she allowed him to lead her into the garden of the cottage, towards a wooden bench which was partly swamped by bamboo grass.

Daisy's taste buds once again twanged with the sharp tang of salt mixed with the scent of the flowers in the air, and as she breathed it in deeply, the remaining frustration of the past hour melted away and she experienced a rush of happiness at being there.

'I love this place,' she burst out. 'It's so great to be here with everyone.'

Adam was looking at her steadily and the air suddenly seemed to change in weight around them.

'Sit down a minute, Daisy, will you?'

Daisy's heart began to race. Feeling a bit shaky, she sat on the bench and Adam sat down next to her, nervously brushing his hair away from his face.

Every sense in her body shouted, *Uh oh!*

Adam took an audible breath. 'The thing is, Daisy, I really like you... I mean *really* like you... as more than just a friend.' He couldn't look at her now and seemed to be trembling.

Her heart went out to him, even though she felt sick with nerves at hearing this from someone she'd known since she was a little girl.

'I just wanted to know, er, if you fancied coming to visit me sometime in Bristol? To see if we could make a relationship – a proper relationship – work.' He turned to catch her eye now, his expression worried. 'I know this must all seem a bit sudden and it's not great timing when you're just about to start uni, but I figured if I don't do it now, you'll meet someone in your first week there and I'll have missed my chance,' he rushed on before she had time to respond. 'I've been wanting to tell you how I feel about you for a really long time but I've never had the courage to do it before. I didn't want to ruin what we have.'

There was a beat of silence while Daisy desperately groped around for something to say.

'I had no idea you felt like that. That's so... flattering,' was all she could come up with.

Though if she really thought about it, of course, and examined everything she'd seen and heard from him tonight, she *might* just conclude that she did have *some* idea...

She really liked him too, always had, but she'd never thought of him as boyfriend material before.

She did find him attractive though, and he was one of the sweetest people she'd ever met. And at least he treated her like an adult and not some annoying little kid, like Zach did.

The thought of Zach and his disdainful frowns helped her to make up her mind about Adam's proposal. Perhaps she should give it a chance. It wasn't as if she had men breaking down the door to take her out and she definitely didn't want to lose him as a friend by rejecting him out of hand.

'Okay,' she said slowly, 'that would be really nice.'

Adam smiled, relief flooding his face. He looked at her hard for a moment and the expression in his eyes made her heartbeat pick up again. Before she had time to think, he leant towards her and kissed her gently on the lips.

Daisy's mouth tingled in response, her blood starting to zing around her body.

He deepened the kiss, his tongue sliding gently against hers and she sank into it, her senses reeling.

Quelle surprise.

He was a good kisser.

His lips were soft, but there was good, confident pressure from his mouth on hers.

And he tasted great.

In fact, to her surprise, kissing Adam felt really quite lovely. Not quite as all-consuming as she thought a kiss should, but nice, safe, extremely pleasant.

'What the hell are you two up to out here in the dark?' came a deep voice from a few feet away.

Daisy pulled away from the kiss, her heart thumping, to see Zach standing there, a look of pure comedic horror on his face.

'Nothing,' she and Adam said in unison, moving away from each other in a knee-jerk response to being caught.

Some unsettling feeling, that she couldn't put a name to, twisted through her at Zach seeing her and Adam like this. Regret perhaps? No, more like satisfaction. This would show him that she was a grown, sexually awake woman. A sexually *wanted* woman.

Adam didn't seem to be able to look at his friend.

Daisy just held Zach's stare, insolently.

'Your mum needs you, Daisy,' Zach muttered, turning away from them and striding off back towards the house, his shoulders stiff.

Daisy turned to look at Adam, who just grinned sheepishly at her.

'We'd better go back inside, I suppose,' he said, getting up.

Daisy nodded, following suit in a bit of daze, her insides scrambled.

They walked back in silence to the cottage, the air thick with the unsaid, but before she could step inside, Adam caught her arm, urging her to look at him.

'So, let's arrange for you to come to Bristol soon then?' he asked with hope in his eyes.

For a fleeting moment, Daisy paused to reconsider her options. There was only really one decision if she was to keep her pseudo family intact.

'Sure, let's do it. Maybe once I'm settled at uni,' she said. 'That'd be lovely.'

Though, if she was honest, after seeing the look on Zach's face, she wasn't so sure about it any more. What had made him react so negatively towards them kissing? From the look in his eyes, anyone would think he hated her. Did he think she was going to break his best friend's heart?

He was such an enigma when it came to his feelings. He'd never seemed that interested in her as a person, or so it had felt when they were young. Apart from one summer when she was eleven and he twelve. He'd rescued her from where they'd been climbing a cliff and she'd slipped and broken a bone in her foot and found she wasn't able to climb down or even walk by herself. He'd been attentive and kind and, slinging her arm around his shoulder, had half carried, half dragged her back to the house where they were staying for the summer.

Once she'd come back from the hospital, he'd changed back to the hard, sardonic know-it-all she was used to though and had spent the rest of the holiday alternately berating her for her clumsiness and ignoring her. This had made her sad at the time. The glimmer of how things could be with him when he'd let his guard down had sucked her into a world of want for more of it. Even though she occasionally saw glimpses of this side of him again, he never fully lost the hard shell he'd built around himself again.

When she'd discussed it with her after they'd gone home, Daisy's mum had put this down to his tough upbringing. 'He's been brought up in a very unemotional, male environment, darling, without much love, I'm sad to say. Just ignore him when he's being like that and remember it's his problem, not yours.' This insight had helped her a little and she'd taken her mother's advice and let most of the teasing go without reacting to it after that.

For some reason, this had seemed to inexplicably rile Zach more and he always countered by pushing harder for an emotional response from her.

Boys.

Though he wasn't really one of those any more.

Her mum was in the living room with Sally, finishing off a glass of wine.

'Did you want me, Mum?' Daisy asked, poking her head around the door.

'I just wondered where you were. You didn't come in with Sam and Zach.'

'I went for a walk around the garden with Adam. It's gorgeous out there tonight,' Daisy mumbled, not wanting to catch her mother's eye. Did she have an inkling about what had happened out there? Had Zach said something to her?

Her mum fixed her with a penetrating look as if she was trying to read her mind, then smiled as if she hadn't found anything to worry about. 'Okay. Well, I think everyone's off to bed now. Have you got everything you need?' she asked.

Daisy nodded. 'Yeah. Night, Mum. Night, Sally. See you in the morning.' She turned and left the room, hoping not to bump into Zach on her way to bed.

Luckily for her, he seemed to have already gone to bed himself, so she washed and brushed her teeth then got straight under the covers, feeling like someone had tied her insides into knots.

3

After breakfast the next morning, the parents dragged them all out for 'a fun walk', batting away their excuses of hangovers and, in Sam's case, a general dislike of any kind of walking, especially *fun walking*.

They caught the passenger ferry across the narrow span of water that linked them to the picturesque village of Polruan on the other side. Zach spent the whole journey chatting to Sam, with his back to her, so Daisy was able to lose herself in gazing out at the stunning scenery and listening to the rushing of the water alongside them without concerning herself with actively ignoring him.

Once they'd docked and clambered out of the

boat onto the quay, they strode off up the steep, narrow road that lead them past the dinky, pastel-coloured houses on the main street of the village. Out of breath at the top, they all paused for a minute or two to survey the stunning scene below them.

In the distance, the whitewashed houses that lined the seafront of Fowey gleamed in the steady sunlight, complimented by the brightly coloured sails of the dinghies that travelled slowly up and down the narrow stretch of water and out towards the blue-grey sea.

It really was a magnificent view.

As she drank in the heart-warming sight, Daisy became aware that someone was looking at her. Senses heightened, she turned to find Adam gazing at her, a crooked smile on his face. She knew she should have been pleased by this, but inexplicably, she felt a flash of disappointment. Internally reprimanding herself, she forced a smile back in reply.

'Beautiful,' Adam said, still smiling directly into her eyes.

'Let's get going,' Zach said abruptly, right next to her, pushing so close past her, she stumbled forwards a couple of steps. He marched off, leaving them all standing there, taken by surprise at his grumpy manner.

'I guess he hates "fun walking" too,' Sam muttered under his breath.

Daisy watched Zach go, his tall, muscular frame seemingly tense with purpose.

Shrugging to each other, they followed in the direction he'd taken and soon caught him up at the turning to the narrow road that led down to Pont. The hedges were high on both sides here and the road barely wide enough for two cars, so they walked in single file, watching carefully for signs of any vehicles approaching. Soon, they found a footpath which led away from the road and continued on a shallow gradient downwards towards their destination.

* * *

In the way that English weather tends to do, the day had become overcast now, with a chilly wind rising and Daisy, who had forgotten to bring her waterproof, shivered in her fleece as fat drops of rain began to fall and soak through her clothes. As they walked on, she thought back to that morning to distract herself from the discomfort.

There had been a peculiar tension at the breakfast table, with Zach studiously ignoring her, a dark expression on his face. She wondered whether he was just hungover, but he hadn't drunk as much booze as the rest of them the night before.

'Watching his figure,' Adam had teased when he'd refused a drink in the last couple of rounds.

In response, she in turn hadn't spoken to him either, or even looked at him if she could help it. Adam, on the other hand, had been overly friendly and chatted to her constantly, warming her with praise and charming her with his gentle wit.

If only she were back at that table right now.

Daisy's head had started to throb from the cold but she trudged on miserably, not wanting to complain to the adults when they appeared to be really enjoying themselves.

Luckily, the rain decided to give them a reprieve a few minutes later and the sun even made an appearance, which changed the mood of the walk again.

Without warning, the winding path suddenly opened out to reveal an idyllic-looking scene. A large lake, framed by trees, lay still in the late summer light. The surface like a looking glass, mirrored the sky above it; clouds moving slowly across it giving the impression of enormous fish swimming lazily just below the surface.

Daisy halted in her tracks, awed by the sight.

A small bridge led over a narrow part of the lake and ducks waddled towards them in hope of an offering of breadcrusts.

They spent a while sitting at the edge of the lake gazing at the water, until the cool air against their damp skin forced them back on their walk. Zach and Sam had banded together and Adam seemed to have become her constant companion now – not that she minded too much. It was nice to have attention from someone who genuinely seemed to like her.

Leaving Pont behind, they walked on for another few minutes until they reached a river which could only be crossed by stepping stones. They all jumped across one by one until only Zach and Daisy were left on the bank.

'Go on Dizzy, you first,' Zach muttered, his sharp tone harsh to her ears.

She turned to look at him. This was the first time he'd addressed her directly all day, she realised. He just stared back at her blankly, his face not giving away a single emotion.

'Okay then,' she said, pushing her shoulders back and stepping forwards confidently, determined not to let his unfriendliness bother her.

'Watch your step,' she heard him say behind her, irony heavy in his voice.

She ignored him.

Arrogant idiot.

He'd always been scathing about anything physical she did, as if she was just some silly, weak girl who would fall over her own feet if not watched like a hawk. It had only made her more determined to do everything he did. And then some. This had intensified as they'd got older and she'd regularly get hurt trying to join in with the rowdy games the boys favoured.

Unfortunately, this time his warning was just.

Half way across, her muddy old trainers, which had lost most of their grip on the soles after a year of hard wear, slipped on some damp moss on the middle stone when she jumped onto it. She hung in the air for a moment, her arms wind-milling at her sides, desperately trying to regain her balance.

It was not to be.

In what felt like slow motion, she toppled sideways into the freezing cold water, which immediately soaked through her clothing and filled her shoes. The water was too shallow to fully immerse her head, but she found it hard to pull herself upright because of the weight of her wet clothes and the fact she was already stiff with cold.

She started to panic, her racing heart lodging somewhere in her throat and her breathing coming out in gasps.

'Daisy, don't worry. I'm coming,' she was aware of Zach saying through the cotton wool that seemed to have filled her brain.

He reached her a couple of seconds later and grabbed her by the arm, trying to haul her out of the water. She was flailing around now, unable to right herself as the panic got a stronger grip on her, and she jerked the arm he was holding, which sent him off balance too. With a shout of alarm, he lost his footing and toppled into the water next to her with a resounding splash.

The shock of seeing Zach fall in stopped the on-coming hyperventilation in its tracks and she managed to recover herself enough to sit up. She turned to see him scowling at her, his previously artistically styled hair flattened by the water.

If she hadn't been so cold and miserable, she would have laughed.

The others had no such compunction and a roar of hilarity reached them from the other side of the bank.

Andy and Jack picked their way carefully back over the stones and eventually managed to pull the two of them up out of the water, good naturedly scolding them for their carelessness and trying not to smile at their aggrieved faces.

'I think you two ought to go back to the house and get dry and warm,' Jack suggested, once they'd returned to the bank they'd just been trying to leave, handing Daisy a key to the cottage. 'Get straight into the shower.'

Daisy just nodded miserably, sneaking a look at Zach, who did not look pleased about the turn of events.

'Sorry,' she muttered.

He just glared at her, pushing his hand through his hair so it stuck up in wild peaks.

He still looks sexy, even when he's soaked through and angry, Daisy mused, before shaking the thought from her head. That was exactly what he'd love to think, but he'd never hear it from her.

* * *

The rain started lashing down again as they trudged back in silence, neither one willing to speak first. Daisy was hyper aware of his agitated presence beside her, but was afraid of provoking a tirade of insults if she opened her mouth, so she kept it firmly shut.

When they eventually reached the house, soaking wet and shivering with cold, they found the power had shorted out.

'One of the bulbs must have blown,' Zach said, through clenched teeth. 'So we won't be able to use the showers. I think they're both electric. And there's probably not enough hot water for a bath after everyone used up the tank this morning.'

'Can we fix it?' Daisy asked, immediately feeling a bit stupid for doing so. Of course they could put the power back on; they just needed to find the electricity box.

'We could try the trip switch; it's probably in the cellar,' he replied, his annoyance apparently only just in check.

There was a key in the cellar door but when Zach turned it, then tried the handle, he found it was really stiff to open. Sighing, he braced himself before throwing himself against it until it swung open.

They peered inside.

'Looks pretty creepy down there,' Daisy ventured.

He rolled his eyes at her then started to descend the stairs. Half way down, he turned back.

'Make yourself useful and look for a torch,' he said gruffly.

'Okay,' she said through gritted teeth.

She went back to the kitchen and rummaged through the cupboards and drawers until she found a Maglite at the back of the cupboard under the sink. She tried it to make sure it was working then took it down to the cellar. It was almost pitch black and freezing cold down there and she shivered hard in her still damp clothes.

As she reached the bottom stair, a draft must have caught the door because it slammed shut behind her with a loud bang.

She froze in horror, then hurried back up the stairs to try and open it, an icy dread sinking through her body.

Nope. It wasn't budging. It was stuck.

'For God's sake, Dizzy!' Zach said, his voice reverberating with annoyance.

'I didn't do it on purpose! A breeze must have caught it,' she said back crossly.

Following her back up the stairs, he tried yanking on the handle too, but it stayed stubbornly shut.

'You should have propped it open before you came down.' He let out what sounded like a low growl. 'Really living up to your name at the moment, aren't you?'

Daisy was too worried about being locked in a cold, dark cellar to rise to his jibe this time.

'Shit!' he said, kicking the bottom of the door.

They alternately tried pulling at if for a few more minutes, but it was no good. It wouldn't open.

Daisy was shivering hard now. Her damp clothes lay icy-cold against her body and the draught that had caught the door felt bitter as it swirled around her hands and face.

'What should we do?' she asked, her voice beginning to shake. She wasn't sure if it was just the cold that was doing it, or the fact that she was actually starting to feel quite scared about being trapped in a dank, dark cellar.

It was like something from a horror movie – not her favourite genre.

But at least someone was with her. Even if it was the last person she'd rather be trapped with right now.

'I suppose we'll have to wait for the others to come back,' he said with a loaded sigh.

'I'm freezing,' she muttered through numbing lips.

Zach was shaking with cold too. He took the flashlight out of her hand, which had formed a vice-like grip around it, and shone it around the room.

'Look, there's a blanket over there in the corner. We ought to get these wet clothes off and wrap that around us to get warm before we get hypothermia. Then I'll sort out the trip switch.'

She looked at him with scepticism, one eyebrow raised. 'You're kidding me, right?'

'Okay, then. What's your great suggestion?' he countered.

It did make sense to take their cold, wet clothes off, of course. She was going a bit numb all over by this point and was desperate to get warm again.

'Alright,' she sighed, 'but eyes right, soldier.'

'Diz, I've seen you in a bikini before,' he retorted, putting the flashlight down on the floor on its end so that it illuminated them both with a faint light.

'Yeah, when I was ten. This is slightly different, I think you'll agree.'

Zach gave her a withering look and started to strip down to his underwear. After a moment's contemplation, where she decided she had no choice if she wanted to keep all her fingers and toes intact, Daisy followed suit, albeit unwillingly. She really didn't want him to see her in just her bra and knickers. She was really paranoid about what he'd think of her body, especially as he seemed to take such pride in working out to keep his own so trim, so she felt a flush of embarrassment when he turned to face her.

'Hey! I said no looking!'

'Oh, for God's sake, stop whinging and get in the blanket.'

He'd already pulled it around his shoulders and he opened it up to wrap it around her body too. They stood there for a moment as close as they could get to each other without touching, the material of the blanket scratchy on her skin.

Daisy was so aware of the proximity of his hard torso to hers that her body gave an involuntary shiver. He looked down at her as the cold draught found its way under the blanket, causing her to shiver again.

'This is stupid. Come closer to me; we need to use each other's body heat to get warm. Dizzy, move closer!' At this, he pulled her roughly towards him, wrapping his arms around her back, so their chests were pressed together. Zach began to rub her back slowly in circular motions and she felt warmth start to sweep across her skin.

'Hmmm, that feels good,' she said without thinking, then froze with embarrassment as Zach started to laugh, his body shaking against hers.

'Don't get too excited,' he said.

'Oh, piss off, will you!'

Zach just laughed again.

There followed a tense few moments where neither of them said anything, too focused on their task of getting warm. Or, perhaps of trying to ignore the weirdness of their close proximity to each other.

'Diz, can you rub your hands over my back too. I'm absolutely freezing here!' Zach said suddenly, making Daisy jolt in surprise.

'Alright, alright, keep your knickers on,' she said, as she began to move her hands over his back. She felt his muscles shift under his skin as he adjusted his stance.

Zach stared down at her steadily. 'Don't worry, I intend to.'

Daisy rolled her eyes, but couldn't bring herself to maintain eye contact. She was glad at that moment that the torch barely threw out any light so he couldn't see how pink her cheeks were.

'I hope there aren't any spiders down here,' she said, trying to change the subject. The feeling of his body against hers was making her jittery now but she could feel the blood start to pump around her body, warming her through, so she didn't move away.

'You're such a girl,' he scoffed.

'Thanks so much for noticing.'

'Bit hard not to with your breasts pressed up against me.'

Daisy started to pull away in anger at this, but Zach was holding her too tightly.

'Touchy, touchy. Stay where you are. This is working,' he commanded, tightening his grip and pressing her even closer to him.

For a moment, she just listened to his breathing, which seemed to be increasing in speed.

Suddenly, she felt his body tense and he shifted his position so that there was more of a gap between their lower torsos and he moved his hands up to jerkily rub her shoulders and the tops of her arms, his gaze somewhere over her head.

'Why are you moving away from me? I'm colder now,' she asked, frowning up at him.

Zach's expression had turned shifty.

Oh.

Her heart started to race. 'Oh my God, you boys

are ridiculous. You only have to mention the word "breasts" and you become randy dogs.'

'Sod off.' It was Zach's turn to get cross now.

'Well, it's true.'

'What would you know about it, anyway? You're still a virgin,' he said, frowning down at her.

Daisy spluttered in humiliation. 'How do you know? I could have slept with loads of people,' she said defiantly.

She hadn't, of course. Not a single one.

'It's obvious. You only have to look at you to know how inexperienced you are. You've got an aura of naivety about you,' he said, his mouth twisted into a wry smile.

Angry heat flooded through her and she tore her gaze away.

'You're such a prick, Zach. I've never met anyone who loves himself as much as you do.'

'Well, nobody else is going to.'

Daisy looked up at him again at that. Even though his voice had been jokey, she caught a flash of sadness in his eyes.

They stared at each other, Daisy beginning to regret what she'd said.

'What are you doing anyway, messing with Adam?' Zach asked abruptly.

Daisy was taken aback at the severity of his tone.

'I'm not *messing* with him. I really like him. What's it to you anyway, don't you think I'm good enough for him or something?' she shot back, her body heating with irritation again.

'No, of course not. I just don't think you're the right person for him. He's a great guy, but totally naïve and easily hurt.'

Daisy was shocked to hear him say this. What did he think she was going to do to Adam? She was strong willed, yes, but never cruel. She looked up into Zach's dark eyes and saw – what? Something intangible there, some emotion she couldn't read.

She suddenly had the realisation that Zach might be jealous of her blossoming relationship with Adam. But why would he be? Since they'd first met, he'd made it his mission to let her know how annoying and immature he found her. That she was beneath his notice.

Perhaps that was it. Perhaps he thought she couldn't possibly be attracted to Adam when he was around and that she was using Adam to get back at him for ignoring her.

'Oh really, so who am I the right person for? *You?*' She put as much ridicule into the last word as she could muster, testing him.

He looked away when she said this, a muscle flicking in his jaw. After a beat, he looked back, right into her eyes and said, 'You couldn't handle me.'

Daisy narrowed her eyes. 'Oh *please*. Just because some of those actors you hang out with think you're some kind of hotshot sex god, it doesn't make you one. I've known you for too long to fall for that.'

They glared at each other, both of them now shaking with anger and adrenaline. It was a battle of wills as to who would break the deadlock first.

Daisy was determined to win; she couldn't let Zach get the better of her again. She felt his grip on her arms tighten and her breath caught in her throat. With a jolt, she realised he was leaning in towards her, their faces getting closer, eyes still locked, as if he was daring her to move away first. But Daisy didn't move away. She wasn't going to give in. *No way*. She would show him that she was just as strong as him, just as confident, despite her virginal state. So, she moved forwards too, facing off with him, daring him to keep coming.

Her stomach was doing somersaults now and she was trembling with nerves, as well as cold, but still she didn't pull away.

Zach's mouth was almost touching hers now and she could feel heat coming in waves from his body.

Strangely, she found she couldn't look away. She was mesmerised by the expression in his eyes.

His gaze suddenly seemed to soften and she saw a momentary hesitation, as if he was fighting with himself about something, before he closed the gap between them, crushing his lips against hers.

She stood there, frozen in shock, her whole body seeming to go up in flames as the mind-blowing realisation filtered through to her brain that *Zach was kissing her*.

Not to be outplayed here – at least that's what she told herself – she kissed him back, just as hard.

Zach let out a low moan from his throat at her positive response and forced her lips apart so his tongue could dart inside her mouth.

Even though she hated him, *hated him* and his bloody superior manner, Daisy felt a rush of longing more intense than anything she'd experienced in her life.

His hands slid down her back, dragging her closer to him so she could feel his erection pressing against her stomach.

As much as she despised his recent treatment of her, she couldn't bring herself to break the kiss. Instead, she opened her mouth wider and kissed him back fiercely, running her nails down his spine.

She could feel his heart beating fast against her chest and his hands swept her body, moving lower, until they were stroking her buttocks, then moving on to lightly brush between her thighs. Daisy felt another heady rush of desire and her breath rasped in her throat. Any vestige of willpower she might have thought she had was spiralling away, out of her control...

Then, suddenly – shockingly – Zach broke away and held her at arm's length, taking the blanket's enveloping warmth with him, his breath coming out in hard gasps.

'What's the m-matter?' Daisy stammered. She was desperate to kiss him again; her body felt as if it was on fire and there was an unfamiliar throbbing deep in her pelvis, urging her on. She needed this to continue, was desperate for it.

'I, um...' Zach appeared to be uncharacteristically lost for words.

'Can't *you* handle it?' Daisy murmured, looking at him directly, holding his gaze. She'd never seen him so out of control before and was fascinated by the change in him. She'd finally discovered that she had some power over him after all.

He was obviously fighting with himself about the wisdom of doing this and she was determined not to make it easy for him. Instinctively, she reached out a hand and, keeping her gaze locked with his, pressed it against his chest, then moved it lower to gently stroke her fingertips, down, down to his lean hips where a dark v of hair disappeared into his boxers, admiring the deep lines and undulations of his torso as his muscles flexed under her touch.

He stared at her for a moment, his eyes veiled and dark, then seemingly made up his mind about something. Moving his hands up to her shoulders, he hooked his thumbs into the straps of her bra and slid them down her arms, pulling the cups down with them to expose her chest. Daisy only managed to draw in a ragged breath before he brought his mouth back down to hers again, his hands moving to cup her exposed breasts.

She felt a rush, like pure electricity, fizz through her body, all her senses alive with the intensity of it. Her insides were like molten lava, the heat reaching its peak in her centre and sending tendrils of longing twisting through her body. She was on fire, lost in waves of pleasure. It was like nothing she'd ever felt before.

There was no going back from this now. She wanted this feeling to go on and on, more than she'd ever wanted anything in her life.

All worries about her sexual innocence deserted her and she felt suddenly wanton and powerful at the way he was reacting to her.

Seemingly, she wasn't the only one because he moved even closer and the force of his body against hers caused her to stumble backwards against the wall.

She let out a gasp at the shock of the cold against her skin.

Grabbing the blanket before it slipped off his shoulders, Zach stepped away from her for a moment.

She felt the loss of his body keenly and almost reached for him to come back to her until she realised what he was doing.

He'd turned to spread the blanket out on the floor next to them and spun back around and grabbed her in a bear hug.

Realising what he wanted, she allowed him to lower her to the floor, so she was lying on the blanket, with him kneeling above her.

She gazed up at him, lost in a world of lust.

He moved so his knee pushed between her legs, opening her thighs so he could slide between them and fit his body against hers.

His gaze stayed fixed on her eyes, searching their depths.

'Okay...?' he murmured, asking for her consent, pleading for it.

'Yes. Do it,' she urged breathily, daring him, revelling in this newfound power. She looked back into his eyes and saw they were fierce with lust, just as she guessed hers must be.

Moving slowly down her body, he kissed first her neck then across her breasts, taking her swollen nipples gently into his mouth, then sucking down, causing her to take a sharp intake of breath. His fingers brushed gently against her mound through the material of her knickers, making her cry out with the need to be touched more intimately there.

Zach raised his head for a moment to look at her, his eyes searching hers again.

'Do it,' she repeated.

He gently hooked his fingers into the band of her knickers and pushed them down her legs, his fingers exploring the skin of her inner thighs as he did so and sending a pulse of sheer desire straight through her. His hands moved back up now to explore the apex of her legs, his fingers stroking, probing and opening her up to him.

She arched her body towards him, desperate for

his touch to go deeper. Reading her body language, he moved the pad of his thumb to gently caress her clitoris, circling her there and generating waves of pure bliss.

A low moan escaped from her throat.

She needed him inside her, couldn't bear it any longer that he wasn't.

She felt him withdraw and the air moved around her as he discarded his boxers before she once again felt his solid body, hard against hers, lining up with her. Slowly and with care, he pushed himself inside her.

For a second, she felt a sharp pain, which made her suck in her breath hard.

Zach stilled and looked down at her, his face suddenly a picture of concern.

'Am I hurting you?' His voice shook, she guessed with the effort of stopping himself going any further.

The pain had subsided now though and was giving way to the most wonderful feeling of completeness. She wanted him to be deeper, right there in the centre of her, continuing the waves of pleasure she was already addicted to.

'No. Don't stop,' she begged, wrapping her legs around his back and pulling him closer to her, gently rocking him, taking him deeper and deeper as she opened up to take the length of him inside her.

'Wait, slow down,' he said, but she silenced him with a kiss, running her tongue along the underside of his top lip, then biting his bottom lip gently. She wasn't in the mood for slow.

Zach groaned and seemingly lost the fight with himself to keep things steady, thrusting into her instead and surprising her with his depth.

She loved it, though. *Loved it.*

They moved together now, a little out of rhythm with each other to begin with, but soon finding a happy medium, rocking and melting into each other, their bodies slick with a sweat they'd worked up between them, despite the cold of the cellar.

As he continued to move inside her, she began to lose herself in the waves of pleasure he was drawing from her, which radiated from her core, every nerve jangling with sensation.

The whole of her skin felt bathed in heat.

She raked her nails across his back as a swell of feeling began to work its way from deep inside her. All those hours of thinking about him, those small frissons of need to see him and the nervy excitement he'd provoked in her whenever he was around, were now culminating in this moment. She arched her back, desperate to get closer to him, for the feeling he was drawing from her to become more intense, more real. She was spiralling down, down, the waves taking her along on their journey.

'Oh, God,' Zach murmured. 'This feels so fucking good.'

She felt another involuntary moan escape from her throat as he increased the pace and moved rhythmically inside her, doubling, tripling the waves of pleasure. She pushed her pelvis higher so each one of his thrusts rubbed him harder against the neediest part of her, building on the blissful feeling there, until it finally crested, her body exploding with pleasure. She was floating, consumed by ecstasy and was barely aware of Zach's breathing becoming faster next to her ear, until he suddenly shouted out her name – her actual name – and shuddered into his own orgasm above her.

She was totally spent. A jellified mess beneath him.

They held each other close for what felt to Daisy like eons, but could only have been less than a minute, the aftershock of their lovemaking still resonating through her body. Eventually, Zach raised his head and looked at her.

'Shit, Daisy, I'm so sorry. I couldn't stop,' he muttered, looking aghast.

Daisy stared at him, bewildered. 'What are you talking about? I didn't want you to stop.'

He withdrew from her carefully and sat up, turning his back to her, the muscles across his shoulders taut.

She felt the sudden loss of his body like she was missing a piece of her own.

'Are you okay?' he asked in a weirdly brisk manner, which caught her totally off guard. She reeled at the coolness in his tone. What had happened to the Zach of a few minutes ago, who had such passion and fierce longing for her in his eyes?

She was suddenly supremely conscious of her nakedness and pulled the edge of the blanket up to cover herself.

'I'm fine,' she said. 'What's wrong?'

'I'm sorry. I got carried away. I couldn't stop myself,' he repeated, his manner so matter-of-fact, it made her take a sharp breath.

Daisy was stupefied by his sudden change in attitude towards her. He'd always been the one on top of every situation and she guessed he wasn't willing to let her get the better of him now either, not when he'd just made himself so vulnerable. He'd been hesitant to have sex with her, she now realised, now she was no longer under the thrall of her libido. He'd been trying to hold back, uncertain about it.

A shocking thought suddenly occurred to her.

'Was that your first time too?' she asked, incredulously.

Zach turned to look at her, then quickly turned away again, but not before she caught the caged look in his eyes.

'It was, wasn't it! And all this time you've let me believe you've slept with loads of women. But I was the first! Ahh! I don't believe this, Zach, after all those times you ridiculed me for being immature.'

'Yeah, well... I wanted it to be with the right person at the right time.'

A rush of disbelief flooded through her. He regretted it. He *bloody* regretted it.

'You fucked that up then, didn't you,' she spat out.

She couldn't believe it. He still thought of her as a kid: someone to protect. Not the strong, confident woman she was becoming.

'We didn't use a condom,' he said, his voice tinged with alarm now.

Heat rushed through her. *Jeez*, she hadn't even thought about that. *Idiot*. She took a calming breath.

'Well, as we've just established, we were both virgins so no STIs. And I've been on the pill since I was fourteen for painful periods, so no babies on the way either. No need to panic.'

He breathed out heavily. 'Thank fuck for that.'

His relief at there being no further complications stung her though. Practically, she knew it was good that they didn't need to worry, but his focus being on that, rather than how she was feeling right now, hurt her deeply.

She guessed at that moment he was more concerned about making sure his budding career as a big shot actor wasn't in jeopardy.

The realisation that he was being a heartless shit must have occurred to him too because he turned back to her and said, 'Look, I really am sorry. I shouldn't have let it happen.'

This admission only served to wound her more.

Tears sprang to her eyes and she struggled up off the ground, grabbing her clothes and pulling them on as quickly as she could, which wasn't easy as they were still damp and freezing cold.

She needed to get back at him, to hurt him like he was hurting her, to protect her dignity.

'Was this all just a ploy to get into my knickers? I bet it was. Cos I'm an easy target, aren't I? Stupid, naïve Dizzy, she won't put up a fight! Have you got some sort of bet on with Adam to see who manages to fuck me first or something? It wouldn't surprise me,' she ranted, the humiliation now turning to anger.

Zach was frowning. 'It wasn't like that. This has got nothing to do with Adam.' He reached out and touched her arm. 'Daisy, don't say anything to him. Please.' He looked imploringly at her now.

Snatching her arm away from his touch, she shook her head in disgust. 'Of course I won't. What do you think I am: stupid?'

He began to say something but she cut him off. 'Don't answer that. God, I hate you, you smug, arrogant bastard! Will you *please* get dressed! Someone might find us at any moment, and the last thing I want is for anyone to know that I had sex with *you*.' She spat this last word out in anger. Because she *did* feel stupid now. How could she have let this happen?

Infuriatingly, even through her haze of bitter humiliation, looking at him now, his expression set in a scowl and his sleek, toned body taut with fury, she still felt a rush of longing for him.

'You didn't seem to mind a minute ago,' he bit out.

'Yeah, well, I was clearly out of my mind too,' she countered.

Zach's jaw was set in a hard line as he gathered his clothes together and pulled them on.

'And don't expect it to happen again. I want you to stay away from me, okay,' Daisy said, her voice breaking with emotion.

She felt a bit nauseous, now it was beginning to hit home what she'd just done.

Poor Adam.

'Don't worry, *princess*, if you think I'm coming within ten feet of you again, you've got another think coming!' Zach hissed back at her.

'Fine!'

'Fine!' They shouted at each other.

Daisy went and sat on the top step by the cellar door, her arms wrapped around her for comfort, her fingers pressed against her swollen lips and tried to ignore the low throb that still resided inside her.

Zach stayed down on the floor of the cellar, glaring at the wall. After a few minutes, he roused himself and went to find the fuse box, flipping the trip switch back to restore the power.

After what seemed like an age, they heard the others come back into the house and Daisy banged on the door until Jack managed to force it open and let them out.

The boys thought it was hilarious that they'd locked themselves in the cellar and made a tirade of jokes at their expense. Sally was aghast at the state of them and ordered them both to have a hot shower immediately.

No-one seemed to notice the frosty atmosphere between her and Zach and she was glad when later, after she was warm and dry again, Sam dragged him and Adam off to play pool at the pub for the rest of the evening.

Daisy locked herself in her room and had a good cry, her treacherous body still craving the feel of him inside her. She could still smell his scent on her too and took another long shower to try to wash him away, gently smoothing soap over her bruised thighs, which to her annoyance only served to heighten the feeling of longing that just wouldn't *bloody go away*.

She was so humiliated at his rejection of her, but also totally confused about how much she still wanted him.

Right there and then, she made a promise to herself to never lose control of a situation like that ever again.

4

Daisy and Zach spent the rest of the long weekend assiduously avoiding each other.

The night after 'it' happened, Daisy had a disturbing dream in which he appeared and held her to him, like she was the most precious thing in the world, and she woke up in the morning feeling, sad, aroused and even more confused. Frustratingly, after that, whenever he came within any kind of distance of her, she felt her deceitful body ache for him, and had to remove herself before she gave in to the feeling and dragged him away to ask him whether he'd really meant what he'd said.

She couldn't even look him in the face any more

though, so there was no way that was going to happen.

To make matters worse, Adam had taken to following her around doggedly. She managed to avoid letting him kiss her again, making sure there was always someone else around when she was with him, but she was keenly aware he could sense that she wasn't as happy about their agreement as she had been a few nights before.

Daisy felt dreadful about being so hot and cold with him and tried to make an extra effort to be friendly – though not too friendly – even though she mostly craved solitude in order to lick her wounds.

Adam eventually broached the subject of her change in attitude to him on their last night there. They were sitting in the pub again, watching Zach and Sam playing pool, Daisy trying hard not to think about what had happened with Zach, when Adam leant in to her and whispered that he wanted to talk to her on her own.

'What about?' Daisy asked anxiously. She was really afraid Zach had let something slip about their encounter and she was frantic that no-one else should know anything about it.

'Just come for a walk with me, will you?' Adam pleaded, his expression grave.

Heart thumping, Daisy agreed, knowing she needed to deal with this sometime and now was probably as good a time as any. She got up and followed him out towards the pub's beer garden.

She imagined she could feel Zach's eyes boring into her back as she left and, turning just before the door, she saw she was right. He was giving her a look so intense, she thought it would pierce her.

Shaken by the ferocity of it and feeling another confusing swell of arousal, she gave him a cool stare back, intent on appearing outwardly aloof. She wasn't about to let him get to her now. Keeping her head high, she followed Adam out of the pub door and into the mild night air.

'Have I done something to upset you?' Adam asked her, when they'd reached one of the picnic tables in the garden and sat down.

Daisy was so relieved this wasn't about Zach, she laughed at the frown on his face.

'Of course not, I'm just a bit tired, that's all,' she half lied.

Adam's frown disappeared. 'You poor thing. It must be awful getting up at lunchtime and spending most of the day either on the beach or in the pub. Exhausting!' he teased, then leant forwards and kissed her gently.

Confused about what the hell to do for the best in that moment, she kissed him back with as much fervour as she could muster, which turned out to be quite a bit once she let herself sink into it. He really was a good kisser and right then, she craved comfort so much, it made her ache.

He drew back and smiled at her and she felt a bit less awful for a second, but only a second, because the feeling of relief was swiftly followed by a sting of guilt. As much as she loved being around Adam, she really couldn't take advantage of his misplaced kindness, not after the way she'd behaved. She really shouldn't let him think everything was okay with them when she was so mixed up about what had happened with Zach.

'Listen, Adam, I've been thinking. Perhaps it's not such a good idea for me to come and see you in Bristol.' She looked at him tentatively, waiting for the fallout.

As predicted, his face fell at her announcement, suddenly a picture of confused shock.

'It's not that I don't like you or find you attractive, I really do, but I don't think I could handle a long-distance relationship. Not when I'm just starting at uni.'

She felt dreadful, but she knew it wouldn't work

out with him right now, not when she felt the way she did about his best friend. She wanted to be able to escape from *the angst of Zach* once at university and she didn't need Adam reminding her of him all the time.

'What did I do wrong?' he asked glumly.

'Nothing, I swear. I'm so sorry.' Daisy went to take his hand, but he pulled it away.

'Yeah, whatever, Daisy.' He got up and walked away from her, his head dipped and his arms folded protectively across his chest.

'Wait, Adam, I really am sorry...' she said to his retreating back.

But he didn't respond, just kept walking until he vanished into the dark.

Daisy was so angry with herself, she kicked the table leg, nearly breaking her toe. Getting up, she hopped around in pain for a while, cursing herself, Zach, Adam, the unfairness of the world, before dropping heavily back onto the seat and burying her face in her hands. How had she got herself into this mess?

How?

* * *

Finally, the holiday came to a close.

Daisy was so relieved to be getting away from the bad atmosphere between her and Zach that she had her suitcase packed the night before, which was unusually organised for her, and woke up early the next morning ready to leave straight away.

Unfortunately, everyone else seemed to be trying to stretch their last morning out as much as possible and sat around breakfasting for an hour, idly chatting.

At one point, she noticed Zach trying to catch her eye whilst she was chomping down on a piece of toast and choked on it until she was red in the face and her eyes streamed. Adam seemed to be ignoring her now, but Sam patted her on the back until she was able to compose herself again.

Daisy left them all finishing their breakfast and retreated to her room, flinging herself onto the bed and screwing her eyes shut in self-disgust. How typical, to make a fool of herself in front of Zach like that *again*.

God, she hated him.

No, not him. Not really. She hated the way he made her feel: like she'd acted like a lush who was now beneath his contempt. But he'd been just as into it as she had, she was sure of it.

Just as she thought this, there was a knock on her door. Her heart sank. She just wanted to be left alone for a few minutes to be miserable in peace, but it seemed it was not to be.

'Come in,' she said resignedly. The door was pushed open to reveal Zach, who frowned at her, as if it was *her* that was bothering *him*.

'What do you want?' Daisy asked, sitting up and experiencing the now familiar rush of longing at the sight of him.

His hair was still rumpled from sleep and just looking at his lithe body, leaning confidently against the doorframe, gave her goosebumps.

The tension in the air lay thick between them.

'Look,' he started, then took a breath and blew it out, as if speaking to her was giving him pain. 'I just want you to know that I didn't set it up, okay? I wouldn't do that. I just made a mistake. It never should have happened. Not like that. Not with you.'

Despite his seemingly apologetic words, his voice held the usual sarcastic ring to it and Daisy felt herself grow angry again.

'Just leave me alone, okay? I get that I'm merely a mistake to you and guess what? You are to me too. So, can we please forget it happened. I don't want to talk about it ever again.'

He looked at her for a moment, then went to open his mouth to say something else.

She cut him off. 'I don't need you to "heal me," thanks very much.'

His expression clouded over at this and he clearly decided there wasn't any point saying anything else, so just nodded, then turned and left, slamming the door behind him.

Daisy punched the pillows behind her in agitation until she felt the tension lift a little. Flopping back onto the bed, she lay there for a while staring up at the ceiling, going over what had happened between them. The low throb of lust was quickly being replaced by a sinking feeling at the humiliation she felt about the whole thing now.

It was hopeless.

But at least she was leaving today and wouldn't ever have to see him again if she didn't want to. She was old enough to refuse to come on family holidays now.

The thought of this being the last ever one brought tears to her eyes, which she swiped away with her hand. No. She wasn't going to mope about this. She was stronger than that. Uni would solve all of this angst. She'd be too busy to even think about Zach and the ball of pain that seemed to have taken up residence in the middle of her ribcage.

Her mother called her down a few minutes later and she went to help bundle the luggage into the car.

After saying a hurried goodbye, first to Andy and Sally, then to Sam and finally to Adam, who just muttered a cursory, 'Bye', and walked off, she looked around to see if there was any sign of Zach.

'If you're looking for Zach, he left to get his train already,' Sam said, as she walked out of the living room. 'He said to say goodbye. He didn't want to disturb you.'

Holding back another rush of hot tears, she thanked Sam and gave him one last hard squeeze – at least he was still speaking to her – before going off to find her parents, who were waiting by the car.

It was the most disastrous holiday she'd ever had, she reflected as they set off back to Oxford. She'd somehow managed to anger not one, but two people she cared about a lot, not to mention losing her virginity in a desperate fumble in a cold, damp cellar, instead of joyously in a warm, plush bed, as she'd always hoped.

She didn't regret that it had been with Zach though, not really. Deep down, she recognised she'd always fantasised he might be her first lover. She just wished it had been under better circumstances.

Guilt came back to wallop her in the gut as she remembered the look of abject hurt on Adam's face when she told him she didn't want to pursue a relationship with him after all. She felt utterly wretched about that. She really *did* like him and maybe in other circumstances, they could have made a go of it. She guessed she'd never know now. He probably wouldn't be interested any more now that she'd rejected him.

She spent the whole journey back trying not to burst into tears.

5

PRESENT DAY

'Okay, Lula, your next – very exciting! – guest is waiting to speak to you on line three,' Daisy said, after pressing the intercom button which allowed her to talk to the *Drive Time* presenter in the studio through her headphones, without it being heard by the microphone.

'This is *Drive Time* with Tallulah Lazenby on Flash FM. Stay with us for our exclusive interview with goddess-of-the-silver-screen, Katrina Cross, who's currently starring in the blockbuster *Ten White Doves* now showing in cinemas.'

Tallulah's amazing, rich, smoky voice came over the speaker in the producer's cubicle, which allowed Daisy to hear what was being broadcast at all times.

'She's up next, right after Laura Lucas' latest release.'

Tallulah hit the button on the desk which triggered the song that was lined up to play. Through the glass, Daisy saw her give her a double thumbs up before picking up the line to have a chat with the actor waiting to speak to her on air.

She leaned back in her chair and stretched out her tired back. It had taken her ages to set up the interview with this famously elusive film star. Despite being one of the most popular performers of the time, she gave very few interviews outside the press junkets which she was contracted to do for the film studios. Daisy had been determined to get her for Lula's show and it was somewhat of a coup that she had. Katrina wasn't giving interviews to any other radio stations in the country.

One of the other broadcast assistants, Claire, who had mentored Daisy when she'd first started working at Flash, came into the booth and plonked herself down into the other chair by the desk.

'Good work, Malone. I can't believe you got Katrina bloody Cross on the show. I bet old Boss Man Jezzer nearly wet his knickers when you told him we'd got her,' she said with a grin.

Daisy grinned back. 'I know, right? I can hardly

believe it myself. I must have e-mailed her agent a million times before she said yes. Apparently, she heard one of Tallulah's shows recently and loved it so decided to come on.'

Claire leaned over and picked up a magazine lying on the desk that the previous BA on shift had been reading. She turned it over and studied the front cover.

'Oh, I so would,' she said, fanning herself with her hand and flipping the magazine round to show Daisy the front cover.

Daisy's stomach plummeted as she took in the sight of Zach's face staring broodily back at her. He looked good. Really good.

'I so did,' she murmured, without thinking.

'You *what*?' Claire sat up straighter in her chair and gawped at her.

Daisy's face flamed. *Dammit*. She'd told herself she'd never tell anyone about the 'incident' with Zach. But it seemed her overwrought brain had other ideas.

'Uh, I mean, I would too,' she said, aware how unconvincing her lie sounded.

'No, no, no. You definitely said that you "did". Come on, Daisy, you can't drop a bombshell like that and not give me every single detail.' She folded her arms and stared at her, clearly not intending to budge until Daisy had spilled every last bean.

'Okay. Yes, I did say that.' She held her hands up in surrender. 'We, er, had a – very short-lived – thing years ago. It wasn't anything really. We used to go on holiday together when we were kids. He went to school with Adam and his family always invited him to come along with us.' Her face flamed hotter at the slightly bent-out-of-shape truth.

Claire leaned in closer, intrigued. 'You're a dark horse. Why haven't I heard about this before? If I'd shagged Zach Dryden, you wouldn't be able to shut me up about it.'

Daisy tried to shrug it off, but she could tell Claire wouldn't be fobbed off and would keep pushing till she gave her more juicy gossip. 'To be honest, it's all a bit awkward because he's good friends with Adam. I thought he was into me at the time, but he was just using me to dispose of his virginity. I was a "mistake" apparently. Anyway, I never see him any more. Adam's been to the States to visit him but I wasn't invited. Thank God.'

'Does Adam know about this *liaison*?' Claire asked, rapt.

'No! And you can't tell him. Honestly, if he found

out... well, he wouldn't be happy. Things with me and Adam had just started to develop at that point.'

Claire studied her through narrowed eyes. 'Hmmm, I suppose it's healthy to have some secrets from your boyfriend. Don't worry, my lips are sealed, but you have to promise me, if you're ever in the position to "bump into" Zach again, you have to introduce me? Deal?'

Daisy snorted. 'Yeah, sure. But don't hold your breath. There's no way he'd want to see me again after the way things ended.' She threw her friend a cheeky grin. 'Anyway, I don't think mouthy pissheads are his type.'

Claire punched her playfully on the arm for that. 'Speaking of which, come and find me when you're finished here, okay? I seriously need a drink tonight.'

Daisy nodded, relieved her friend wasn't going to pump her for any more information about Zach. At least not right then. She suspected there would be a further interrogation after a few drinks that evening though. 'Yeah, okay. Be with you once Lula's wrapped up.'

'Good girl.' Claire got up and patted her on the head as she walked past, giving her a backwards wave as she left the cubicle.

As soon as she'd gone, Daisy picked up the magazine and stared at the photo of Zach. Yeah, he still had the same effect on her, even after all this time.

Daisy often thought back to six years before, to the *Zach debacle* as she liked to think of it. After getting back home, she'd been really down about the whole episode for quite a while. She was devastated at the thought that she'd never be able to be part of the old 'holiday family' group again. She'd loved those times with such a passion that the thought of them never happening again cut her to the core.

Luckily, Adam, who apparently was also upset at the thought of never seeing her again, had called her out of the blue one day a few months into her university career and had asked to visit her. He'd come to her student halls and first charmed her flatmates, then charmed her with the most gracious apology and a long monologue about why he couldn't let her go and why he was perfect for her as a partner. She'd listened and decided he was probably right. But mainly, she desperately didn't want to lose him from her life either.

As soon as he'd finished his speech, she'd leant forwards and kissed him, momentarily surprising him with the passion of it, but he'd quickly recovered and kissed her back hungrily.

She decided never to mention what had happened between her and Zach to him though and he seemed satisfied with her explanation that she was confused about where her life was heading when she'd rejected him before and hadn't wanted to complicate things even more by starting a relationship with him at such an unsettled time.

Things had developed from there.

They kept in touch with each other constantly while they were both studying at their respective universities and after she'd graduated, she'd moved to London to pursue a career in the radio industry and he'd followed her there.

By that point, it seemed like a natural step to move in with each other.

It was a really comfortable connection they shared – easy and straight-forward – and she loved him dearly. He was a kind and fun partner and was good at ignoring her occasional black moods and treating her with the tenderness and respect she craved.

The first time they'd had sex, she was really worried about how it would make her feel, after thinking of him almost as a brother for so long, and had asked him to be patient with her. He'd agreed and they'd taken it slowly, building her confidence until she couldn't stand it any longer and had ordered him to make love to her.

Afterwards, he'd held her in his arms and she felt awash with contentment. Adam was a good, considerate lover, but Daisy was acutely aware that he never made her feel the way that Zach had just by looking at her. This kept her affection for him slightly aloof, she realised, but Adam didn't seem to notice and she knew he really meant it when he said he loved her.

Not long after Daisy had started at university, Zach had been offered an acting job in California on a very successful, long-running TV series and so very rarely had time – or perhaps the inclination – to contact anyone at home, so none of them had seen him again after the holiday in Cornwall. Until recently that is, when out of the blue, he invited Adam and Sam to go over to the States to visit him. Even though she told herself she didn't want to see Zach again, she'd found being left out of that visit heart-breaking. Not that she'd let Adam know she'd felt like that.

Letting out a sigh, she threw the magazine back onto the desk and turned her attention back to the show, where Katrina Cross was about to give Flash FM a major boost to its listenership.

At least her life seemed to be finally starting to come together. After years of hard work, for very little pay, she was at a point in her career where she felt confident in her abilities and was being remunerated properly for them. Even better, she was now afforded the longed-for respect that she craved from her colleagues for her professionalism and dedication.

Yeah, life was good.

She was looking forward to the future, with Zach Dryden now very firmly in her past.

6

A week later, Daisy let herself into the Islington flat she rented with Adam, sighing with relief as she felt the warmth from the radiator in the hall soak into her chilled skin. It was bitterly cold outside and she hadn't dressed properly for the weather that morning.

Hanging up her thin, three-quarter length trench coat, she kicked off her kitten heeled boots and walked into the living room, quickly walking out again and grimacing at how messy it was in there. Unfortunately, neither she or Adam were particularly tidy and they'd become even worse at clearing up recently because they'd both been working such long hours – her at the radio station and Adam at the recruitment agency he'd snagged a job with after moving to London.

She went into the kitchen instead to fix herself a well-deserved drink. It had been a tough day. One of the interviewees hadn't turned up when they were supposed to, leaving Jez the Breakfast Show presenter – who was unfortunately also the Station Manager, therefore her boss – to fill with chat and music until she was able to locate the errant politician and get them to speak to Jez over the phone instead. Jez's face was like thunder after the show had finished and he'd said a few choice words to her before leaving for his office. He hated it when things went wrong – not being good at improvising, like Tallulah was, and having an unwieldy ego when it came to his professional reputation – and he always let Daisy know exactly how annoyed he was when they inevitably did.

She poured herself a glass of red wine and leant back against the counter to drink it, only raising the glass part way to her lips before she was distracted by the sound of Adam banging in through the front door, chucking his coat on the floor and kicking his shoes against the skirting board.

Daisy winced at the noise.

He barrelled into the kitchen, taking her glass of wine out of her hand and downing it in one.

'Hey, that was for me,' she protested.

Adam just grinned wickedly.

'Hey, guess what?' he said, reaching behind her for another glass and the red wine bottle and filling both glasses back up. He handed one to her before he continued, smiling at her expectant face.

'I had a phone call from Zach.' He paused for effect. 'He's moving back to England.'

Daisy's stomach lurched. Just the sound of his name still made her heart race and she was intensely aware of her face getting hot.

Turning away, so Adam wouldn't notice the effect his announcement had had on her, she poured a bit more wine into her glass till it was brimming to the top.

Why was she so rattled? It wasn't as if he was moving in with them or anything. She would probably see as little of him as she had previously.

'Anyway,' Adam continued, not seeming to notice how he'd plummeted her into a world of nervous panic, 'he and his girlfriend are coming to stay next weekend.'

Daisy nearly choked on the mouthful of wine she'd just gulped.

'What?' she gasped. *No*, this couldn't be true. She couldn't have him in her home; how would she cope? And even worse, how would she manage, meeting his – what she had to assume would be – gorgeous, glamorous girlfriend.

She groaned inwardly.

'Don't worry, I'll help you tidy up and we can go out for a meal,' Adam said, mistaking her apprehension for a worry about being ready to receive guests in time.

She wracked her brain for a decent excuse to say no which Adam would accept without her giving the game away about how she felt about Zach, but nothing sprang to mind. It was hopeless. There was nothing for it but to tough it out.

'Okay,' she said slowly. 'But you have to promise to help me get the place ready for visitors or I'm off to stay in a hotel for the weekend. By myself!' she stated, pointing her finger at him, to avoid any misunderstanding.

* * *

She spent the next week in a state of high anxiety and the day before they were due, rushed around the house cleaning and tidying like a whirlwind, snapping at Adam if he moved so much as a coaster when she'd 'just bloody put it there!'

'Chill, Daisy, for God's sake,' Adam muttered, when she nearly screamed in frustration at him for dropping crisp crumbs onto her newly vacuumed floor.

When she glared at him in annoyance, he grabbed her in a bear hug and gave her sloppy, wet kisses all over her face until she started to giggle, hyper aware that she really did need to 'chill' or she was going to make Adam suspicious about her behaviour.

She was so intensely nervous about seeing Zach again that she couldn't eat properly and her heart raced every time she thought about him. She must have lost half a stone in weight over it.

Finally, Saturday rolled around and Daisy woke early to shower and spent ages making herself look as good as possible. She needed to somehow arm herself against him and she felt the best way to do this was to put on a protective armour of clothes and make-up. She wanted him to see that she was a serious adult now and not some naïve wimp any more.

She was dreading meeting Zach's girlfriend, who she was sure would be extremely cool and who would make Daisy feel like a complete nerd in comparison.

Her nerves were so jangled, she jolted in shock when the doorbell eventually rang to hail their arrival.

Pretending to read the magazine she'd been staring unseeingly at for the last twenty minutes, she said, 'Get that will you,' to Adam.

He sighed loudly and shook his head at her.

'What?' she said. 'I'm just finishing this article.'

Adam shot her an amused look. 'Calm down, Daisy, it's only Zach. I know he's meant to be some "hot-shot actor" now,' he put this in air quotes, 'but he'll still be the same sarcastic, irascible bastard we knew when we were young.' He gave her a quick, reassuring kiss on the head and went to answer the door.

That's what I'm afraid of.

As soon as Adam left, she stood up and checked her appearance in the mirror. Her cheeks were flushed, but apart from that, she thought she looked okay.

Taking up what she hoped was a relaxed-looking position next to the sofa, she listened as Zach's low, rumbling voice greeted Adam at the door, followed by the sound of a drawling, sing-song, American voice.

'Zach, we'd almost given up on you. As usual,' Adam teased. 'Daisy's in the living room. She's just finishing reading an article,' he said, with a layer of sarcasm levelled just for her.

A shiver of anticipation ran through her as she stood ready to greet them.

Taking a deep breath, she tilted her chin up in a show of confidence and plastered what she hoped would come across as a natural, welcoming smile onto her face.

The first person to walk through the door was Zach.

Daisy had never seen him look so good.

He seemed to have grown into his looks even more, if that was possible. His hair was cut into a short, spiky style and his bronze skin had darkened in the California sunshine. His dark eyes crinkled into a smile when he saw her and Daisy felt her legs start to tremble.

Apparently, he still gave off the same fiercely sexual vibe as he'd always done and she found herself lost for words under his gaze.

Zach had no such problem and walked straight

over, putting his arms around her and drawing her against his body. 'Hello, Dizzy, how are you?' he said, into her hair. He then moved his mouth lower so he was speaking directly into her ear. 'I'm sorry. Adam insisted we come and I couldn't think of a good enough reason to refuse,' he murmured, so only she could hear him.

He pulled back to look her in the face, his smile warm and assured, as if he was just exchanging pleasantries with an old friend that he'd not seen for ages. This was for Adam's benefit, she guessed.

He really was an excellent actor.

'Yes, I'm fine, thanks. Um, how are you?' She appreciated the apology, but didn't know quite how to feel about it. So, he wanted to be here as little as she wanted him here?

His body, in such close proximity to hers, was causing frissons of long forgotten need to spiral through her.

She cursed her jumpiness. The last thing she wanted was for him to think she was still affected in any way by him.

'I'm great, thanks. This is Lola,' he said, turning to indicate the woman who had followed him into the room. She was, of course, absolutely beautiful. A sheet of strawberry-blonde hair fell around her slender shoulders and her bright-green eyes gave

Daisy an inquisitive, appraising look before she smiled at her.

'Hey there, I've heard so much about you,' she said, in a melodic southern States accent.

Daisy just smiled back weakly, feeling even dowdier than she'd anticipated.

'Anyone fancy a cup of tea?' asked Adam, breaking the strange atmosphere.

'I'll have Earl Grey, no milk, no sugar,' said Lola, turning to beam at Adam, who, by the look of him, seemed entirely enchanted by her mesmerising exquisiteness.

'Just an ordinary one for me: milk, two sugars. Thanks, Ad,' Zach said.

'Okay, back in a sec,' Adam said, dragging his gaze away from Lola to leave the room.

Daisy frowned after him. 'Er, feel free to sit down,' she said to Zach and Lola, who were hovering by the sofa, 'and tell me what you've been up to.'

'Oh, well, Zach's been incredibly busy, the poor darling, finishing up the show,' Lola jumped in, delicately positioning herself on the sofa cushions and drawing her legs up in a becoming, model-like pose. 'It's a good job we work together because otherwise we'd probably never see each other,' she drawled, her gaze wandering around the room, taking in the rather worn furniture and faded decoration, her nose just the tiniest bit wrinkled. 'Been here a long time, have you?' she asked.

'A couple of years,' Daisy replied. Lola's condescension was already making her hackles rise.

Just chill, she's probably really nice and just a bit nervous about meeting Zach's oldest friends.

'Hmm,' said Lola, without interest, turning to smile at Zach. 'Are you okay, darling, not too tired from the drive?' she asked, running her brightly painted nails down his arm.

'I'm fine,' Zach answered gruffly, not meeting her eye. He turned to Daisy. 'So, Diz, where are you working at the moment?'

'Flash FM. I'm a broadcast assistant, but training to be a producer,' Daisy said.

'Oh yeah? What does that involve?' he asked.

Daisy started to describe her job to him, aware the whole time of how unglamorous it must seem compared to the life he and Lola had been living in the States. She kept stumbling over her words and was acutely aware of Lola staring at her, her eyebrows raised.

Luckily, she was saved from further humiliation by Adam returning with the tea.

'Here we go. So, Zach,' he said leaning over to

pass the cups around, 'how come you're moving back to England now?'

'I've been offered a part in a play in London, which is the perfect move for my career right now. I've missed acting on the stage. And, to be honest, I've missed being here too. California's great, but England's my real home.' He took a sip of his tea in contemplation.

'And have you got a job lined up too, Lola?' Adam asked, his eyes appearing to wander momentarily from her perfectly made up face to her pert breasts.

'Not yet, darling, but I'm sure something will come up soon. I just couldn't bear to be so far away from Zach.' She turned and gazed at Zach with a look of absolute adoration.

Daisy wished she could turn to Adam and covertly pretend to stick her fingers down her throat at the sickliness of this. How could Zach, of all people, possibly fall for someone as superficial as this? Or was she being a bitch? Maybe she was just jealous of Lola's utter confidence in herself. She really must try harder to be nicer. She barely knew the woman, after all.

'So, I've booked this great restaurant for tonight,' Adam said, clearly also feeling the need to change the trajectory of the conversation. 'It's just round the corner, so not far to walk.'

'Round the corner from *here*?' Lola said with what sounded very much like distaste.

'Yes.'

'Oh.'

'Listen, Adam, why don't I make a call and get us into The Acer tonight,' Zach suggested.

'Don't you have to book months in advance to get in there?' Adam pointed out.

'I don't,' Zach said, seemingly without ego.

Adam frowned. 'It's a bit expensive for my tastes.'

'Don't be so tight,' Zach said, punching him on the arm. 'It'll be great. I've heard the food's amazing. Seven o'clock okay with everyone? My body clock's still out of kilter and I get hungry early.'

When everyone nodded their agreement, he left the room for a minute to make the call and they all sipped their tea until he came back in, giving a sage nod. 'Sorted. They're blocking us a table.'

'Good,' said Lola, seeming to relax for the first time since they'd arrived.

Daisy guessed this was because she was finally getting back to doing the type of things she considered acceptable in the course of her amazing celebrity life.

'Hey, did Adam tell you, I managed to snag an interview with Katrina Cross for my radio station?' Daisy asked Zach, suddenly feeling an urge to prove to everyone that she was a success at her job too.

'We know Katrina, don't we, babe?' Lola said. 'Don't you share an agent with her?'

Adam cleared his throat. 'What a coincidence. I told you there must be greater powers at work, Daisy.'

And with a sinking feeling, Daisy realised what had happened here. Adam had asked Zach for help and he'd agreed.

'Did you—?' she started to ask Zach, but found she couldn't quite get the words out. How humiliating. Especially when she'd been boasting to everyone that she'd managed to make it happen all by herself.

'Adam mentioned you were trying to book her for an interview,' Zach said, looking shifty now. 'I was just trying to help a friend.'

She swallowed hard, desperately trying not to let her humiliation show on her face. 'Right. Well, thanks... That was... good of you.'

Zach smiled, accepting her thanks, but she could tell from the expression on his face that he realised she wasn't entirely happy about him butting into her career.

'Let's go for a wander around the local area,' Adam suggested, clapping his hands on his knees and getting up off the sofa. 'We can show you the sights.'

Lola wrinkled her nose at this too, but she was outvoted when both Zach and Daisy got up and went to put their shoes on, breaking the tense atmosphere that hung like a bad smell in the room.

* * *

They spent the rest of the afternoon showing Lola and Zach around their little corner of London, people turning to stare at the beautiful and highly recognisable couple wherever they went.

As predicted, Islington didn't impress Lola one bit and she kept talking about how much better everything was in California and complaining about how cold it was in England.

'You'd better get used to it, sweetheart,' Zach said. 'Now we're here.'

Lola pulled a face, but didn't contradict him.

She supposed this must be what Zach had always wanted: a beautiful, submissive girlfriend to hang on his arm and make him feel good about himself.

No wonder she and him had never got on well together.

They were all looking round a large, independent furniture shop that Daisy loved because of its ever-changing, eclectic collection of stock, when Adam excused himself to take a work call.

'At the weekend?' Daisy muttered under her breath to him, annoyed that he was leaving her on her own with Zach and Lola.

'I'll only be a little while, but I can't ignore this. It's my boss,' he said. 'If I'm not back in half an hour, I'll see you at the restaurant.'

Daisy sighed and nodded in resigned agreement.

Heading off to find where Zach and Lola had got to, she heard low voices coming from behind a large bookcase at the far end of the shop.

Stopping in her tracks when she heard her name, she took a couple of paces backwards so they wouldn't see her and hovered there for a minute to listen to what they were saying, feeling a bit naughty, but absolutely compelled to do it. She was fascinated to know what they were like together when they thought they were alone.

'It's funny because I didn't think you had any female friends. You told me you don't believe in them. "Men can't have women as friends. They always want to screw them." That's exactly what you said, word for word, as I remember,' Lola said, in an accusatory voice.

'Yeah, well, Daisy's different.' Zach's voice was unmistakable in its gruffness.

'Because you've already slept with her?'

There was a long moment of silence.

'You have, haven't you? Don't lie to me. You know I can read you like a book.'

Daisy held her breath, grimly intrigued to hear what he was about to say.

'Yeah.'

Lola let out a rather unbecoming snort. 'I knew it. I could tell the moment I saw you awkwardly hugging her.' She paused for a minute. 'Does Adam know?'

'No.' His voice was full of tension now.

'Was she with him at the time?'

'No. Well... sort of... Look, it shouldn't have happened. I felt really shitty about it afterwards.'

'What, you just couldn't help yourself? Even though she was with your best friend?'

'Yeah, well, I'm not proud of it.' Zach sounded

genuinely anguished, which sent a shiver of disquiet down Daisy's spine.

'Hah! All these secrets you've been keeping from me. Is there anything else I should know?' Lola asked, archly.

'No.'

'What was it about her that made you do it?' There was a loaded pause. 'Don't tell me. She was so sweet and innocent, you just had to corrupt her?'

Zach let out a frustrated groan at that. 'Look, we'd been friends since we were kids. She intrigued me. And yes, I guess in my youthful ignorance, I wanted to corrupt her. But half of me wanted to protect her as well.'

'You were in love with her, weren't you?' Lola said in a shocked-sounding voice.

It was at this moment that the sales assistant decided to make an appearance and stride over to where Daisy was lurking to ask if she needed any help with anything.

'Er, no, I'm fine, thanks,' Daisy muttered, her heart in her mouth as Lola's final words rang in her ears. That couldn't be true. *Could it?*

Shooting the assistant a tense smile, she walked quickly away on shaky legs, back towards the shop's entrance, hoping to God that Zach and Lola hadn't twigged that she'd been eavesdropping on their conversation.

When they both appeared a minute later, finding her staring blindly at some curtain poles that she had absolutely no interest in, Zach gave her a cautious-looking smile.

'You okay, Diz?' he asked, raising an eyebrow at her, perhaps because of her choice of object of fascination. At least she hoped so.

'Yes, fine. Perhaps we'd better go, though. They probably don't keep the tables in this fancy restaurant of yours if you're late. Adam's going to meet us there. He had to sort out something for work.' She could barely look at him.

He nodded, his eyes hooded and his gaze intense, as if he was trying to translate a hidden meaning in that statement. 'Okay,' he said, 'then let's go.'

Daisy saw Lola grasp his hand as they exited the shop onto the high street. 'As if they'd give our table away,' she muttered with utter derision.

Daisy stiffened, but decided to shake it off. She guessed she was even further up Lola's shit list now if the woman believed Zach had been in love with her at one time. Even if it had to be complete nonsense. It had to be.

Didn't it?

Daisy hailed the next cab that was passing and they all clambered in – Zach giving the address of the restaurant in Covent Garden – and she spent the whole journey there trying not to look at either of them and give away her nerves about what she'd overheard in the shop.

* * *

Adam was waiting for them outside the restaurant when they arrived and they all piled inside, Zach speaking to the maître d' and getting them taken straight to their table at the back.

Heads turned as they walked through the diners, but neither Zach or Lola reacted to the stares and whispers. Daisy wondered how they coped with being looked at as much as they were. It would drive her introverted-self insane.

Once at the table, Lola made a fuss about where they were being sat, complaining she could 'see the bathroom door' from where she was sitting, so Zach asked to move tables, which the staff kindly accommodated, but nothing, it seemed, was good enough for Lola. She spent the whole time complaining about the service and the lack of choice of good wines.

To Daisy's disgust, Zach just let her rant on.

They managed to polish off three bottles of wine between them and by the end of the meal, despite Lola's grumbles, Daisy found herself happily tipsy and entranced by Zach's stories about his life in California. As he talked on, she found it increasingly difficult to drag her eyes away from him and only realised she'd been staring at him when Adam repeated a question that he'd asked her.

'Daisy, I said do you want any dessert?'

'Hmm?' She was finding it a bit difficult to focus now. Her head was swimming. 'No, no, I'm fine. I think I'll just nip to the ladies though.'

'I'll come too,' said Lola, to Daisy's dismay.

'Okay,' she said, as brightly as she could manage, trying to manoeuvre her way out of the table without upsetting the glasses and plates. 'I think it's this way.' She led Lola off in the direction of the bathrooms, trying not to stumble.

'So,' Lola said, turning to Daisy and blocking her way into the cubicle as soon as they got in there, 'Zach tells me you two had a bit of thing at one time.'

Daisy was totally taken aback by her brazenness in addressing it like this. Were all Americans this confident? The thought made her feel ridiculously British and uptight.

'What... what did he say?' she asked, even though she knew. She was still hoping the two of them hadn't realised it was her lurking behind that bookcase.

'Oh, just that you were a bit besotted with him when you were younger and he thought you were sweet, but had to let you down gently.' She smiled coolly at Daisy, the lie tripping off her tongue so easily.

Another excellent actor.

'Did he?' Daisy said, aiming for nonchalance, despite her rising temperature. She was aware that Lola was goading her, but she was damned if she was going to give her any kind of reaction. 'Well, it was a long time ago when we were both very young and stupid. Excuse me, I need to pee,' she said pushing past Lola into a cubicle and shutting the door.

'I can see why you fell for him, sweetheart,' came Lola's voice, floating under the door. 'He is gorgeous. Great body. Exciting to be around. Spectacular in bed.' There was a loaded pause. 'I'm expecting him to propose any day now and I'm just gonna have to say yes.' This was followed by a tinkling laugh.

Daisy's stomach plummeted and her skin

prickled all over, like she was being jabbed with pins.

Surely not.

She somehow managed to clear her painfully constricted throat and say, 'That's great, congratulations,' in a jolly sounding voice, even though what she wanted to do was throw open the door and vomit all over Lola's six-inch, designer heels.

After taking a moment to calm herself, she exited the cubicle to find Lola studying herself in the mirror, dabbing her lips with a tissue.

'Want some lipstick?' she asked Daisy. 'It would really brighten your face up. You're a pretty girl. You should make the most of your looks.'

Daisy was so taken aback by the passive-aggressive dig that she just stood there gawping at her for a moment, before pulling herself together.

'No thanks,' she managed to struggle out.

Keep calm and ignore her, she told herself, *she's probably feeling insecure about your past with Zach.* But as Lola shrugged and turned to leave, Daisy couldn't stop herself sticking her middle finger up at her back. Even though she knew it was childish, it made her feel mildly better for a moment.

When they got back to the table, Lola leaned down and gave Zach a long kiss on the lips before

sliding in next to him and draping her arms posses-
sively around his shoulders.

Daisy smiled at Adam as she sat back down and
he returned her grin, adding in a grimace and the
smallest of jerks of his head towards where Lola sat,
wrapped around Zach.

So she wasn't the only one to find her annoying.
The realisation warmed her. Good old reliable
Adam. At least he was on her side.

After what seemed like an eternity, and another
bottle of wine, they finally paid for their meal, splitting it two ways between each couple, Daisy trying
not to let her eyes water at the cost. When Adam
suggested they take the Tube home, Lola looked
aghast. 'In these shoes!' she exclaimed. So, a taxi
it was.

Daisy got the impression she was used to always
getting what she wanted, though incredibly, even
this win wasn't good enough for Lola and she com-
plained loudly all the way back about how badly the
cab smelled and how she always travelled in limos
'back home'.

Daisy covertly rolled her eyes at Adam and he
just smiled patiently back at her.

As they stumbled into the house, Lola let out a
loud yawn and announced she was going straight to

bed. 'Jet lag,' she said, as if it was an affliction to be pitied.

'I'll show you where you are,' Adam offered.

'That's my bag there,' she said to Adam, pointing at it. Turning back, she looked pointedly at Zach. 'Are you coming, darling?' From her tone, it was clearly more an order than a question.

'I'll be there in a bit. I'm going to have a nightcap first,' he replied firmly.

This was obviously not the answer Lola wanted to hear and she turned in a huff and followed Adam, who had picked up her bag as instructed and was leading the way to her room.

Zach just ignored her and walked into the living room.

'You don't mind fetching me a drink, do you, Diz? I feel like getting totally blasted tonight,' he said with a sigh, landing heavily on the sofa.

Daisy frowned at him, curious about his sudden change in mood. He'd seemed fine in the restaurant.

'Are you okay?' She sat down tentatively on the sofa, next to him, but not too close.

He snorted. 'What do you think?' Raising his eyebrows, he jerked his head in the direction Lola had disappeared. 'I'm sorry about her,' he said with a sigh. 'She's being an absolute fucking nightmare, but

I just don't seem to be able to shake her off. She won't take no for an answer. I thought if I moved back to England, she'd finally get the message and leave me alone, but she's even prepared to follow me over here. I'm just hoping she'll miss California so much, she'll decide to go home.' He sighed again, looking suddenly very tired.

Daisy couldn't suppress her grin of relief.

Zach looked up at her, frowning at this show of mirth.

'All right, Miss Perfect, there's no need to gloat,' he said in annoyance.

'I'm sorry, I know it's not funny but it's really tickled me,' Daisy said, breaking into laughter.

After a moment, Zach started to laugh too, staring down at the floor in front of him.

'I know, what a fucking loser. I can't even get my girlfriend to leave me.'

'So, you're not going to ask her to marry you then?' she asked him hesitantly.

'What?' he said sharply, jerking his head round to look at her. 'Is that what she said to you? Oh shit.'

Daisy laughed again at his pained expression. She'd never been so relieved about something in her life.

'Dizzy, if you don't stop laughing at me, I'm going

to have to resort to drastic measures to wipe that grin off your face.'

He was looking at her steadily now with his dark, penetrating gaze, and she experienced a sudden rush of desire, her body heating in the most intimate of places as her pulse began to race.

She stared back at him, her alcohol-fuddled brain slow to catch up with exactly what was going on here.

What was he going to do?

Out of nowhere, she had a sudden, desperate need for him to kiss her.

'Diz, about what happened last time I saw you —' he began, shifting closer to her, but was interrupted by Adam returning, stumbling a little as he came into the room. He'd polished off the rest of the wine in the bottle just before they'd left the restaurant and it seemed to be taking its toll on him now.

'Anyone fancy a drink? I think we've got shhume whisky in the kitchen,' he slurred, looking between them both.

'Sure, that would be great,' Zach said, casually moving away from Daisy.

'Okay. Jussht going for a pisshh first, then I'll get them.'

Adam walked away, leaving them both looking anywhere but at each other.

'So, you and Adam are happy then?' Zach asked suddenly, breaking the tense atmosphere that had descended on them.

Daisy felt a swell of disappointment that they weren't going to carry on with the conversation he'd started to broach.

'Yes, very happy, thanks,' she said automatically. But even as she said it, she knew she didn't sound as convincing as she should have. If she was being honest with herself, their relationship had felt a lot more like friends with benefits for a while now. And even then, they'd both been so busy and tired from work recently they'd not actually had sex much.

But they definitely cared very deeply about each other and treated each other with respect. They were good together.

Unlike her and Zach.

She looked at him sitting there and thought how much she still wanted him, but how much of a mistake it would be to get involved in any way with him again.

He was wrong for her.

She needed stability.

Someone she could trust to look after her.

And she had very little self-control whenever he was around, which made her nervous.

It seemed similar thoughts were going through his head too, because he appeared to give himself a little shake and stared down with a frown at the sofa cushion between them.

'Look. I really just wanted to apologise for how I acted on that holiday in Fowey. I was completely out of order and I treated you like shit,' he said. 'You're a good friend and I miss you.'

He glanced up to see how she was taking this admission.

In all honesty, she was stunned. She hadn't expected such a heartfelt apology from him.

'It's okay,' she whispered, her voice seeming reluctant to work now. 'We were both a little out of our minds, I think,' she said with a grim smile.

'Can we have a friendly hug and move on from it?' he asked gently.

The thought of touching him right now set her head in a spin, but she couldn't refuse if they really were making up as friends. And she did want to be his friend again. She missed him too – so much it ached.

'Of course.' Moving closer to him, she let him

gather her up in his arms, trying not to breathe in the delicious, intensely familiar scent of him.

'Thank you,' he murmured into her hair, as if it genuinely meant a lot to him that he had her forgiveness and her friendship back too.

She felt him kiss the top of her head, then down near her ear, smoothing his fingers over her hair as he did so.

It was a strangely intimate feeling. Like he cared for her. Like he loved her.

Her body gave an unaccustomed throb and she pulled away from his grip to look him in the eye.

He looked back at her with an unreadable expression.

The air was still around them, like time had frozen.

Daisy felt her breath catch in her throat.

Then, without warning, Zach brought his mouth down against hers.

An immediate wave of longing ripped through her.

She opened her lips a little to draw in a shaky breath and he took the opportunity to slide his tongue into her mouth.

The taste of him was *divine*.

He kissed her hard, running his fingers back into her hair and holding her head so she couldn't move.

Not that she wanted to.

His lips were soft, but the pressure against her mouth was firm and oh, so very welcome. All thoughts spun right out of her head as she kissed him back, sliding her tongue against his, pushing it deep into his mouth and revelling in the intoxicating *rightness* of it. Like this, right here, was where she'd always craved to be.

Drawing back just a fraction from her, he moved his head to kiss her from a different angle, running his tongue along the inside of her top lip, then gently biting down on her bottom one, just like she'd done to him all those years ago in the cellar.

'Oh, God, Diz, I've been wanting to kiss you all fucking day,' he breathed against her mouth.

There was a loud clunk outside in the hall and Zach quickly drew away from her, a look of alarm on his face. He got up and left the living room to see what the noise had been.

Daisy's head was spinning. She felt charged with adrenaline, but the thought that Adam might have seen them made her shiver with fear.

She suddenly felt too drunk, as if the adrenaline had hyper-charged the alcohol in her system.

'Are you okay, mate?' she heard Zach ask.

'Yeah, fine, I just tripped over your bag and dropped one of the glasses,' she heard Adam reply.

Thank God, Daisy thought. She felt a rush of shame at the idea of Adam catching them kissing.

How could they have been so *stupid*? And, more to the point, how could she even think of doing this to him? In his own home. What kind of a selfish bitch was she?

By the time Adam and Zach had cleared up the mess and returned with fresh drinks and the now half full bottle of whisky, she'd made up her mind to tell Zach he had to leave her alone. And she him. It was the only decent thing to do. Clearly, they couldn't be friends.

No matter how bereft that left her.

As she watched him come back into the room, she became aware of tears welling in the back of her eyes. Her body craved him – *so much* – but he was bad news. He'd always loved to play with her affections just for the thrill of getting a rise out of her. She wouldn't allow it any more. She couldn't. She liked her life the way it was; she didn't need him messing it up for her again.

He glanced over at her while Adam was putting his drink down on the side table and made a face to reflect his relief too, that they hadn't been caught.

Daisy just glared at him and he seemed taken aback by her sudden coldness.

Adam started rambling on about old times, really slurring his words now as the whisky added to his wine high and Zach joined in, every now and again shooting Daisy questioning looks when he thought Adam wasn't paying attention.

She stayed silent, except for when directly addressed, desperate to get out of the room, but not wanting to make it obvious to either Zach or Adam that she was flailing.

The level of the whisky bottle got lower and lower as they refilled their glasses.

After a decent amount of time had passed, she finally got up.

'I have to go to bed. I'm really tired.' She made a move towards the door.

Zach knocked back his whisky in one gulp and stood up too. 'Diz, can you show me where the bathroom is?' he asked, already walking towards her. 'I'll be back in a sec, Ad, mate.'

'Sure, no problem, *mate*,' Daisy heard Adam reply and she turned back to look through the open doorway and saw him close his eyes and sink back onto the sofa in a drunken daze. He hadn't sounded angry though, so she guessed, with a surge of guilt-tinged relief, that he really hadn't seen them kissing earlier.

Unable to unpick her racing thoughts right now, she stumbled down the corridor towards the bathroom, intensely aware of Zach's presence behind her.

As soon as they reached the door, he wrapped his hand around her arm and pulled her inside, closing the door behind them. It was dark in there, but she could just make out his outline moving towards her and she backed away, trembling, until her legs hit the side of the bath.

'Diz, I'm sorry. I never meant to put you in this position and I love Adam like a brother, but you and I... we're meant to be together. I think you know it too. There's always been this *thing* between us.' He cupped her face with both hands and leant towards her so their lips were practically touching. 'I know you feel it too,' he murmured against her mouth, the haze of whisky on his breath making her heady.

They were both drunk, she realised, and out of their minds. Again.

A slow, sinking sadness worked its way through her chest, followed by a torrent of guilt. 'No. I won't do that to Adam. I can't play your games any more. This is my *life* you're messing with.'

Zach was silent for a moment, his breathing shallow. 'You belong with me, Daisy, not him. We were each other's firsts. I'm yours and you're mine,' he said, his grip tightening on her jaw as the frustration grew in his voice. '*Mine.*'

Daisy jerked her head back, out of his grip, anger flaring in her chest. 'I do *not* belong with you. You're just drunk and too much of a coward to end your relationship with Lola, like a *grown up.*' She put her hands flat against his chest and pushed him away from her so he had to take a stumbling step backwards. 'How can you treat me like this? Like I'm some kind of pet to play with? I want you out of my house, first thing in the morning and I don't think we should see each other again,' she hissed, her voice starting to break with emotion. She couldn't deal with this; she was too knotted up inside.

Zach let out a low sigh, as if he was intensely disappointed in her. 'If that's what you want, Dizzy, that's fine with me.'

Stepping away from her, he turned and opened the door, walking back out into the corridor and heading, she supposed, back to Adam in the living room. Or maybe to his bedroom and Lola's warm, willing body.

Daisy stood there, trembling with disbelief, staring into the darkness, unable to comprehend everything that had just happened. She felt like screaming. Instead, she pulled herself together, brushed her teeth with a trembling hand and went to her room. Pulling off her clothes and throwing them onto the floor, she climbed under the duvet, her head buzzing.

After ten minutes of lying there, tossing and turning, she heard Adam come in to the bedroom, undress and get into bed next to her. He snuggled in close.

'Are you okay, babe?' he whispered into her ear in a slurred voice, stroking her arm and moving his hand down to cup her breast.

'Adam, I'm really drunk and tired. I'm not in the mood, okay,' she said, and felt his body stiffen next to her. She'd never denied him sex before.

'Sure. Okay,' he said in a hurt tone, before turning away from her with a huff.

Daisy sighed. How had it come to this? Why could she not just be friendly with Zach without having a desperate need to either touch him or fight with him all the time – and he her, it would seem? He really was the bane of her life.

And the bloody arrogance of the guy, thinking she somehow belonged to him, just because he was her first lover.

She fumed silently for a while before eventually dropping off into a troubled sleep.

* * *

When she woke the next morning, to her relief, Zach and Lola had gone, leaving a scribbled note to say they'd had an urgent call from Lola's agent and they'd had to go and meet him as soon as possible. They hadn't wanted to wake them up to tell them this.

'Ugh, who'd be an actor! Meetings on a Sunday, for God's sake!' said Adam groggily, when Daisy brought the note into the bedroom to read to him.

Daisy just felt numb.

7

It had been a year, almost to the day, that she'd last seen Zach, when Daisy came home from work to find Adam sitting at the kitchen table in a bemused state, his mobile in front of him.

'Hello stranger. I wasn't expecting you back till late again. Did the office burn down or something?' she asked, dumping her bag on the table.

'Ha. Funny. No. My last meeting was cancelled because Tim went home ill. I thought I'd see if you were around to have dinner with me.'

'Ah, sorry, I'm meeting Claire at the pub. She's having a dating nightmare and needs some moral support.'

'Oh. Okay. No worries.' He stared back down at his phone again, his brows pinched.

'What's up?' she asked. 'You look concerned about something.'

'I just heard from Zach.'

As usual, the sound of his name gave Daisy goosebumps. She worked hard to control her expression, so as not to make the sudden flash of anxiety obvious to Adam.

They hadn't heard from him again after he and Lola had left that morning, but Adam had written it off as Zach being swamped by work and Daisy hadn't tried to disabuse him of the idea. He'd been surprisingly blasé about it, actually, which had surprised her at the time – Zach and Adam had been best friends since childhood, after all – but they now lived very different lives and she guessed Adam had just come to accept this.

'What did he have to say?' she asked, her voice a little unsteady.

Could he really be coming back into her life? Just as she was starting to make peace with what had happened and get used to the idea of never seeing him again? He seemed to have a knack of knowing the moment she started to feel okay about losing him as a friend.

'He apologised for not being in contact. He said the play fell through and he went back to the States almost immediately after visiting us. Apparently, he was offered a role in a film that he just couldn't turn down there, so postponed his plan to move back to England. Oh, and he split up with Lola, didn't say why. Sounds like he's got the pick of a new partner since his show did so well though. I have to admit, I'm pretty jealous,' he said with a slow wink, to show her he wasn't serious.

Daisy slapped him playfully on the arm.

He grinned and pulled her towards him, onto his knee, wrapping his arms around her and squeezing her till she shrieked.

'Get off, Adam, you're hurting me, you oaf!' she gasped.

He released her and as soon as her arms were free, she squeezed his cheeks hard in retaliation, laughing at how absurd he looked.

'What?' he said through squished lips. 'Come here and give me a kiss.' And he moved towards her, making wet kissing sounds.

'You are ridiculous!' she said through her giggles, pushing him away. Getting up, she walked towards the fridge to get the milk out for a cup of tea.

'So Zach just called for a catch-up chat, did he?

He's left it an awfully long time to remember his old friends,' she said, with her back to Adam so he wouldn't see how hard she was finding it to talk about Zach without it showing on her face.

She knew she wasn't being altogether fair; they hadn't tried to contact him either. For good reason on her part.

'Well, he didn't just call to say hi,' Adam said. He paused for effect before saying, 'He's invited us to his film's premiere at the Cannes film festival next month. Apparently, his studio will put us up for free in a hotel for the week and pay for the flights.'

Daisy's stomach lurched. 'Do you think we should go?' she asked hesitantly, willing him to say no.

'Well, he did act like a massive prick the last time we saw him, but if he's willing to make it up to us with a free holiday...?' He shrugged. 'We probably wouldn't see much of him anyway. He'll be with his "acting buddies" most of the time.' He looked at her, seeming to be gauging her reaction.

Adam had to be the one to lead this, she realised. It would look strange if she pushed too hard to either go, or not go, so she just nodded and smiled.

'I guess we'd be crazy to turn it down when we can't afford a holiday like that ourselves right now,' he said, still sounding a bit unsure and looking at her intently. 'What do you think?'

She took a breath while she thought about it.

It would be a good opportunity to see Zach again and maybe clear the air, once and for all, so she could stop thinking about him and what happened the last time they saw each other. If that's what she wanted.

But did she?

And at the Cannes film festival of all places. She'd always wanted to go to that and soak up the atmosphere and now she was being given the chance. With someone on the inside too, which most people never had the opportunity to experience. Perhaps she could use it to get interviews with some famous people for the radio station, if she played it right.

But could she do that?

Or should she tell Adam he had to go on his own and let things rest with Zach?

But she knew, even as she thought this, that of course she would go. She couldn't not see him, despite how it might make her feel. Anyway, he was drunk last time they clashed and in the throes of a break up with Lola, so can't have been thinking straight. It would be very different this time.

Plus, she was a whole year older and wiser and felt she could handle herself better.

'Yeah... okay. I'll have to see if I can get the time off work first, but it could be fun. I've always wanted to go to Cannes with you,' she said, cringing a little at twisting the truth.

Adam didn't seem to notice though and nodded. 'Okay, then. I'll let him know it's a yes.'

He walked over and kissed her on the forehead before going over to fill the kettle for the tea she was about to make. She smiled at him, her mind racing.

She could do this. No problem. She was just going to have to be really strict with herself this time and let Zach know from the off that there was to be no more funny business.

* * *

A month later, Daisy and Adam blinked in the bright French sunshine as they stepped out of the plane and onto the steps which would lead them down to the landing strip, then onto a bus that was waiting to take them to the airport terminal.

Flying into Nice airport had been eye-opening. Daisy had gasped in excitement as the plane had banked and flown low over the brilliant azure sea and golden sand of the Nice coastline. The strip where they'd begun to make their descent had seemed awfully narrow and for a moment, Daisy had held her breath in anticipation of something going wrong. It hadn't though; they'd had a good landing, if a touch bumpy, and coasted to a stop a little way from the hangar.

Adam had slept for the entire journey, falling into a slumber before the plane had even begun to taxi down the runway. Daisy was always jealous of how easily he fell asleep. She found it almost impossible to nap unless she was cosy and warm and lying down flat.

After making it down the rather shaky feeling steps from the plane, Adam stretched out his arms and yawned, catching Daisy across the ear.

'Ouch, you klutz!' she muttered.

'Sorry, sweetheart,' Adam replied, not sounding sorry at all.

Daisy bristled at the affectionate term. She hated being called sweetheart, or darling or any other simpering term of endearment. Or maybe it was just the way that Adam said it that got her back up.

Breathe, she told herself, *you're on holiday.*

Ever since she'd learned they would be going to Cannes – and more to the point, that they'd be seeing Zach again – she'd been in a state of constant nervous agitation.

In fact, in the last few days before they left, she'd been so wound up, she'd started making mistakes at work, which was a real no-no in her book.

Once they'd cleared passport control, they went outside to look for the car that was meant to be picking them up and transferring them to where they were staying for the week.

Zach had arranged all the transport at the French end and chosen their hotel. Apparently, the studio was more than happy to pay what must be an extortionate fee during the festival, as Zach was now such a rising star in the movie world he was able to pull a lot of strings.

Daisy had been aware of Zach's continual professional momentum, of course. She knew he'd been in a big-hitting film that had been received really well in England, as well as the States, and this had propelled him to the dizzy heights of Hollywood notoriety.

For a time, he'd seemed to be on the front of every magazine she picked up and the guest of every chat show she tuned in to. As soon as she saw his striking face or heard his deep, gravelly voice, she would hurriedly put down or turn off the offending article. She just couldn't bear to be reminded of him.

Until now.

She'd finally come to terms with the fact that it was time she started making peace with what had happened – or rather hadn't happened – between them. She couldn't allow her hang-ups about him to ruin things for her. It was ridiculous that she couldn't get on with her life without worrying about him springing up at every turn.

And it seemed he wanted to make peace with her too, considering he'd invited her along to Cannes, as well as Adam.

'I can't see anyone holding a card with our names anywhere,' Adam said, breaking into her reverie. 'Wait here, I'm just going to check over there.' He pointed to a limousine with its driver standing by the driver's door.

'Yeah right, Adam, in your dreams!' Daisy said, eyeing the gleaming car. She would love to be driven around in a stretched limo. Cheesy or not, you'd feel really special if one of those pulled up to take you wherever you needed to go.

Adam stopped to talk to the driver of the limo and Daisy was amazed to see him turn round and beckon her over.

'Surely not,' she breathed, when she got to him.

'Oh yes, only the best for us,' Adam said, with a strange edge to his voice.

She looked at him questioningly, but he just grinned back at her.

Shaking her head in amazement, Daisy climbed into the car, thanking the driver for holding the door open for her. She slid along the seat to allow Adam to follow her in, which he did with an exaggerated bounce, nearly propelling her off the seat with his weight. Straightening her skirt in annoyance, she shifted back on the plush leather.

She was soon distracted by how ridiculously opulent it was inside.

There was a big screen directly in front of them which was tuned to a music video channel and along one side of the car, a small bar held a good selection of fine whisky and even an open bottle of champagne.

'Well, there's no point letting this go to waste,' Adam said, reaching for the chilled bottle and a couple of flutes. He poured them both a glass of the pale-golden liquid, handing Daisy hers and clinking his against it.

'Cheers,' he said and downed it in one.

Daisy rolled her eyes at his boorishness and took a sip of hers. It tasted fantastic.

As the bubbles worked their way to her stomach, she felt the beautiful warmth of the alcohol flooding through her. She'd drunk champagne before, but it had never tasted this good. She smiled over at Adam as she felt a sudden rush of warmth towards him. This was going to be a fun trip. She was determined it would be. They'd both been working way too hard recently without a break and it had started to feel like they were just housemates, rather than girlfriend and boyfriend. Adam was always staying late at work or going out for drinks with his team, which she never got invited to. But then she was just as bad with her all-consuming work and erratic schedule. They'd been ships in the night for quite a while and hadn't found the time or energy to have sex in ages.

So, a few days away together would probably do their relationship some good.

Adam appeared to be thinking along the same lines because he smiled back and leant towards her, giving her a big, lip-smacking kiss. 'I'm so glad we're doing this together.' He clinked his glass against hers again, even though his was empty. 'To us.'

'To us,' she repeated.

'Oops, better rectify that,' he said, noticing the

lack of champagne in his glass and pouring himself another.

'Steady on, you don't want to be blind drunk at ten o'clock in the morning,' Daisy chided him.

'Why the hell not? We're on holiday, aren't we?' Adam said with a touch of annoyance.

Daisy sighed. Ever since they'd heard from Zach, it seemed as if they'd both been a little on edge around each other. Was it her guilty conscience playing tricks on her? Or was it just old-fashioned relationship fatigue?

She couldn't deny that her feelings for Adam had waned since they'd first got together – surely every couple's did? – but ever since she'd found out she was going to see Zach again, Adam had started to get on her nerves. The small things he did and said, that she used to find sweet and endearing, had started to grate on her.

She'd noticed a slight withdrawal of his affection towards her too, but had put it down to them both being constantly tired and stressed.

As the first day of the holiday had come closer, Adam had seemed more energised though. He was obviously really looking forward to letting go and enjoying himself.

* * *

Once out of the airport, the limo drove through the suburbs of Nice and out to the autoroute.

Daisy settled back into the seat and watched the scenery flash by. Here, in the south of France, it was very green but with a slightly washed-out look, as if the sun had bleached everything with its intensity. The rushing by of the trees along the autoroute was mesmerising and Daisy found herself deep in thought. What on earth was she going to say to Zach when she saw him? She'd be friendly, but aloof, she decided. He was bound to be just the same: arrogant, self-important and derisive, but she'd have to ignore all that and just enjoy the experience for what it was.

Her skin tingled as she thought about seeing him again, though. She'd have to be very strict with herself. There was no point getting twisted into knots anyway, as Zach was bound to have a myriad of women hanging on his every word.

At the thought of him with other women, she experienced an intense rush of jealousy, like she had when she was young, and quickly shoved the thought to the back of her brain, giving herself a shake.

'Are you okay? Are you cold?' Adam asked,

glancing over at her. 'The air con is a bit fierce in here.' He fiddled with the controls which were on a panel in front of them.

'There, that's better,' he said, settling back into his seat. He put his arm around her and pulled her in tight to him, their earlier snappiness seemingly forgotten.

Daisy gazed up at him. He was such a handsome guy, with his chiselled jawline and bright-blue eyes. A lot of women would be falling over themselves to be with him, Daisy thought to herself. A lot of women *did* fall over in front of him, in fact. He would walk into a room and turn heads, no problem. But for Daisy, he still didn't have the ability to turn her to jelly, as Zach did. Not that that was everything in a relationship. Those sorts of feelings were for short-term flings, not long-term companionship.

'Nearly there,' Adam said suddenly, giving her a squeeze.

They'd left the autoroute and were now driving through the outskirts of Cannes. It seemed a pretty normal place to Daisy, not as swanky or showy as she was expecting – until the limo turned onto the Croisette.

There were crowds and crowds of people thronging the street which ran alongside the beachfront. They passed the Palais des Festivals where the red carpet was already laid out, ready to receive the actors as they made their way to the premiere showing of their film amongst the glare of the media and thousands of adoring fans.

Daisy watched the sunshine play on the waves as they continued along the Croisette. As they slowly moved down the road, hampered by the crowds of people crossing from one side to the other, Daisy gazed at the sea lapping against the beach, her sight line broken occasionally by the enormous boats moored along the docks, and the huge tents along the front, which had been erected to hold the celebration parties for the studios and selected guests once the films had been shown.

It was another world. You could practically smell the wealth in the air.

Facing on to the sea on the other side of the road were the grand hotels which she understood from her research would house the film studio executives and some of the stars of the films. Most of them had bars in their front gardens and these were filled with glamorous-looking people all dressed in the highest of high fashion, sipping cocktails and chatting to each other, their eyes hidden behind enormous sunglasses.

Daisy looked down at herself and felt like a frump in comparison. She realised with a lurch that she hadn't packed very well for the holiday. Most of the clothes she'd brought were just plain shorts or skirts and vest tops, nowhere near the designer fare that was on show here.

Just as she finished this train of thought, the limo turned into one of the huge hotels which over-looked the sea, its sweeping driveway flanked by movie billboards. Daisy felt a shock of recognition as she noticed Zach's broodingly handsome face looking out from one of them above the film's title, *Damascus Days*. She glanced away quickly, looking for a distraction. Her eyes alighted on the sign on the hotel.

'The Carlton!' Daisy read in surprise. She was sure she'd heard that this was one of the places the movie stars stayed. Surely, *they* weren't staying here?

'We must be meeting Zach here before we're shuffled off to our skanky hotel in the burbs,' Adam said with a raised eyebrow.

The limo pulled round to the front entrance and the driver opened Daisy's door for her.

'Are we meeting Zach Dryden here, then going on to our hotel?' she asked him, as she climbed out as gracefully as she could, aware that there were a number of people watching to see who would emerge from the limo, hoping to spot a famous face.

'No, Mademoiselle, you're staying 'ere, I believe,' he replied in a thick, French accent, offering her a hand as she straightened up.

'Oh my,' was all she could muster. The driver went round to get the bags out of the boot as Adam climbed out too. 'Did you hear that? We're staying here!' she said to him, unable to keep the quiver of excitement out of her voice.

'All right, be cool,' Adam admonished, looking around as two stunning and very elegantly dressed ladies passed by, giving him an appreciative look.

Daisy rolled her eyes at him and followed the driver, laden down with their bags, in through the front doors of the hotel.

It took them only minutes to check in at the lavish reception and they were whisked upstairs to their room in a plush lift by a very efficient bell boy. At the door, Adam gave him a five-euro note as a tip, trying to look as if he stayed in this type of hotel all the time.

'Whoa, look at this place. It's bigger than our whole flat,' Adam said with awe in his voice.

Daisy smiled to herself and shook her head. Well, this was not what she was expecting at all.

There was more complimentary champagne in the huge, plushily furnished room, which Adam opened and helped himself to. He handed her a full glass and motioned for her to drink up.

'I could get used to this,' he said, drinking half of his own in one gulp.

She sighed in wonder, looking around and taking in the Belle Epoque furnishings and the long French windows that led out onto a balcony overlooking the sea.

Well, this was certainly going to be an experience.

8

By the time Zach called to say he was on his way to see them, Adam had polished off the bottle of champagne and called down to reception for another one to be sent up, much to Daisy's annoyance.

She'd spent the time unpacking her suitcase and glumly looking through her clothes, willing them to be more stylish and better suited to what appeared to be the most upmarket film festival in the world.

She'd known it would be a glamorous scene, but had felt that her down to earth but tasteful clothes would be fine for the few days they were staying.

Now, as she stared through the window at the crowds of elegant couples parading along the Croisette, she knew she was well out of her league.

What on earth would she wear for the premiere of Zach's film and the party afterwards? Admittedly, she'd packed in a bit of a hurry, after being delayed at work the night before and not having time in the morning to review her choices because of the early check in time at the airport. Her standard little black dress had seemed fine at the time, but as she looked at it now, she noticed how faded it had become from being worn so much and that the hem was starting to come unstitched. She mentally checked her bank account and came up wanting. She just couldn't afford to splash out on a designer frock at the moment.

Oh well, it's not as if anyone's going to be interested in me, what with all these famous Hollywood types floating around.

Now as she gazed at Zach, who had just arrived at their door looking as handsome and charismatic as ever, she felt dowdy and out of touch.

How had that happened?

She didn't usually have a problem with her looks or style, but being here in the presence of so much wealth and elegance, she felt like she didn't come up to scratch.

Zach didn't seem to notice how frozen her smile was though because he strode right over to her and hugged her close to him, as if that awful scene between them all those months ago had never happened.

Her head swam as she breathed in his scent – his natural smell, not from a bottle – that she remembered only too well. She'd occasionally thought she caught his scent in the air, at the most random of times: in the studio on her own, in a friend's car on the way to the theatre, even once just walking down the street on her way to the local shop for a bar of chocolate. Each time, it had brought her up short, desperate to locate its source and flooding her with memories of their time together.

He pulled away and looked down at her. 'Hello Diz, it's great to see you again.'

He hadn't changed a bit. His dark eyes smiled into hers, twisting her stomach into knots.

Giving herself a mental shake, she made herself reply. 'It's great to see you too.'

Zach turned to look for Adam. He was standing by the window now, looking at them with a taught, hard expression on his face. Ignoring this, Zach marched over, clapping him on the back and flashing his devastating smile.

'I'm sorry it's been so long since we've seen each other. I've really missed you both,' he said, turning back to Daisy.

Adam didn't reply, which was unusual for him.

Daisy frowned at him, but he just looked back, blankly.

'Adam's been on the free champagne since the airport,' she said, apologetically, glaring at him and trying to motion a response with her eyebrows.

'Yeah, it's a good tipple this. Expensive,' Adam finally said. 'Thanks.'

'No problem.' Zach replied, looking over at Daisy with a questioning frown. She raised her eyebrows in bewilderment. 'So,' Zach said, choosing to ignore Adam's strange mood, 'I've got some great stuff lined up for us to do.'

He actually seemed excited at the prospect of spending some time with them, Daisy was surprised to discover.

'I've found this fantastic little restaurant; it's off the beaten track so it won't be swamped by hangers-on.'

Adam snorted in derision at this and Zach turned to look at him.

'Sorry, Ad, but to be frank, the place is swarming with people trying to make it in the business and they're only here to make contacts. It's primarily a business conference, but with a lot of glamorous events attached because of the nature of the beast.'

Adam raised his eyebrows. 'The *beast*. That's about right.'

'The thing is,' Zach continued, ignoring his friend's sarcasm, 'because I have a recognisable face, it's tricky to get out and show you around without being mobbed. I don't mean to be a dick about it, but it's a major downside of being an actor,' he concluded, looking over at Adam with an entreating look on his face. 'Come on, Ad, you know me. I don't care about all the fame shit. I really love what I do but it can be a pain in the arse to have everything you do put on social media. I know,' he held up both hands, palms forwards, 'I picked this life, but give me a fucking break, please?'

Adam folded his arms. 'You've changed so much since we were kids. I hardly recognise you any more.'

Zach walked over to him and put a hand on his shoulder, looking directly into his face.

'Look, I know I acted like an arrogant arsehole the last time you saw me. I was in the middle of a messy break up with Lola and being out in LA amongst all the false adoration had warped my brain. I'm sorry, okay? I really wanted you both to be here to celebrate with me this week; you're my oldest and best friends. I promise never to act like that around you again.' He looked over at Daisy now.

'Please?' he said, his expression pleading. 'I need the two of you to keep me grounded.'

Daisy couldn't help but feel for him. He appeared to be completely genuine in his request for their support. He didn't have family like they did, she reminded herself. Only them.

'Of course we forgive you. We've all known each other far too long to stop being friends now.' She looked over at Adam for agreement. 'Right, Adam?'

Adam sighed and nodded, a slow smile spreading across his face. 'Sure,' he said. 'You'd be fucked without us,' he teased, walking over and punching Zach on the arm.

Daisy saw Zach wince at the power of the blow, but he held his head high and pulled Adam into a gruff embrace.

'Great. Now that embarrassing shit's over, let's get drunk,' Adam said, walking over to the fresh bottle of champagne that had been delivered by room service a few minutes before. Before Daisy or Zach could say anything, he loosened the cork and sent it flying across the room with a loud pop.

Adam smiled wickedly at them both before putting the bottle to his lips and taking a long pull. Zach turned to Daisy, a frown marring his brow. 'Is he okay?' he mouthed, looking back in consternation as Adam started to choke on the bubbles.

Daisy shrugged covertly, not wanting Adam to see they were discussing him behind his back. Zach turned back to his friend and grabbed the bottle out of his hand.

'Give me that. It's my turn,' he said and took a big swig himself. He handed it to Daisy. She shook her head and put it back in the ice bucket.

'Hey,' Adam said, 'I haven't finished with that.' And he picked the bottle back up and threw himself onto the deep, squashy cushions on the sofa. Some of the champagne sloshed out of the bottle and Daisy winced and sucked in a breath as it landed on the expensive-looking material.

Adam ignored her.

'So, what time's dinner?' he asked Zach, who was watching him with a worried frown.

'I'll pick you up here at eight,' he said. Then turning to Daisy, he motioned for her to follow him to the door.

'See you later,' Adam called from the sofa, slumping back and raising the bottle to his lips again.

'God, I'm sorry,' Daisy said, as she and Zach

walked out into the corridor and out of Adam's earshot. 'I don't know what's got into him.'

'Ah, don't worry,' Zach said. 'He's probably just blowing off some steam. I did act like a total prick last time I was around him. He must have hated me for going on about my "perfect" life so much. He's been such a good friend to me and I haven't treated him well, especially recently,' he finished with a knowing look. Daisy felt herself growing hot just thinking about what he was referring to.

'Yeah, I guess he's within his rights to be a bit pissed off with you, especially when the last time we saw you, you were too busy playing the big shot to consider anybody else's feelings,' she said, folding her arms. 'Like making us go to that ridiculously expensive restaurant when he'd already booked somewhere. You really embarrassed him.'

She knew she was projecting her own guilt about their last encounter onto him, but right at that moment, she didn't care. Her shame and anger needed an outlet.

To her surprise, Zach just laughed. 'That's what I love about you, Dizzy. You always tell it to me straight. I respect that. You don't pander to my moods like everyone else. I think it's because you're not scared of me?' He raised his eyebrows in question.

She tilted her head in contemplation, then nodded in agreement. Yeah, he was probably on the money with that. Fear was the one emotion she didn't encounter when it came to Zach.

'It's a good feeling,' he murmured, 'being around someone who can see right through your bullshit and still show up for you, even when they have every reason not to.'

At these words, her legs felt suddenly wobbly, so she leant against the wall. 'Yeah, well, there were times when I genuinely felt like I couldn't. But I was still figuring out who I was and how I wanted to play things. How to "do" life, if you know what I mean? Turns out, none of us are perfect,' she said with a grin.

Her heart was racing now, but she also felt serenely calm. It was great to be finally having such an honest conversation with him. Perhaps she *would* be able to be around him without them having a problem this week, after all.

'Well, I'd say you're smashing it. And look, I'm really sorry about interfering with the Katrina Cross interview. That was all ego on my part. I guess I wanted to prove to you there was some good in me, though it ended up being self-serving bullshit in the end.'

She shrugged. 'All water under the bridge.' She leant towards him in a pseudo menacing manner. 'But if you ever get me an exclusive interview again, which boosts my career and reputation, I'll disown you as a friend.'

He grinned back at her.

'But, seriously,' she said, 'please don't try and help me. I really want to do it on my own.'

'Understood and noted,' he said, holding up both hands in surrender.

'And as for the rest of it,' she raised her eyebrows, hoping he'd catch her meaning without actually having to say the words, 'it's all in the past now, right?'

She felt she had to get their relationship straight between them right now if they had any chance at all of remaining friends. Even though she was still drawn to him, she knew he'd be bad for her. He was too transient. Adam, on the other hand, was a kind, loving, steady partner, which was exactly what she needed.

'Absolutely,' he said, with a serious expression on his face now. 'No more messing around. Just friends.'

'So, we're okay then?' she asked, needing to put an end to this conversation now.

'Yeah. We're okay,' he agreed, with a grin.

'Good,' she said, ignoring her usual physical response to that heart-melting smile of his. She was just going to have to train herself out of it. 'See you later then.'

She went back into the room and was about to close the door when Zach called her name and held up his hand in a halting gesture.

'Before I forget, here are your accreditation badges. You'll need them to get into the rest of the festival. Like I said, it's mostly businesses with their stands, but you can go and have a coffee in the UK Film tent or go to any of the showings of upcoming releases in the cinemas, for free.'

'Great,' Daisy said, thinking about all the eavesdropping she was going to be able to do. She'd be able to get a flavour of the film scene for the report on the festival that Jez at Flash FM was keen for her to put together.

She looked more closely at the badges that Zach had handed to her. 'Hang on a sec, where did you get this picture?' Her badge had quite an old photo of her on it. She was smiling at the camera, squinting slightly from the sun in her eyes.

'Oh, yeah,' Zach said, looking at the photo. 'It's from Andy and Sally's anniversary dinner in Fowey. Sally sent it to me after that weekend,' he said, a cagey look in his eye.

'Oh, right,' Daisy said. He'd had it for a long time then. How come she'd never seen it before?

Not that it mattered.

'Thanks, Zach,' she said, giving him a nod.

He nodded back and turned to go.

'See you later,' she said, closing the door.

Back on the sofa, Adam had fallen asleep with the bottle still in his hand, lying precariously across his body, the open neck just starting to tip downwards.

Daisy rescued it before the frothy liquid poured down the back of the sofa and put it back in the champagne bucket.

She sighed. She couldn't understand why Adam was acting like this. Maybe he did need to blow off a bit of steam, as Zach had suggested. He had been working awfully hard recently.

But deep in her gut, she had a niggling feeling that there was more to it than that.

* * *

By lunchtime, Daisy had already taken a stroll along the seafront, down to the Palais de Festival, soaking up the buzzing atmosphere and leaving Adam on the sofa sleeping off all the booze he'd drunk.

She went and had a quick look around the festival to get her bearings, flashing her badge at the people manning the doors. But Zach was right; unless you were working in the film business, it didn't hold much appeal.

She found the UK Film tent that he'd mentioned and sat outside in the little makeshift courtyard drinking black coffee in the sun, listening to the hum of business chatter and gossip happening all around her.

From where she was sitting, she could eavesdrop on a number of conversations coming from the surrounding tables and kept herself amused listening in to the pitches for new films that were being presented by enthusiastic new film-makers to the money men and women.

She tried to keep a straight face as the ideas became more and more preposterous sounding. *I'm bound to see that appear on the cinema next year though,* she thought to herself in amusement.

After polishing off her second coffee, she returned to the hotel for some downtime and to get ready for the evening meal. She'd thought about her conversation with Zach the whole way back, deciding that it was really good to have finally cleared the air between them. She realised that even though she'd been upset at the time and confused about the way she'd lost her virginity to him, she now thought of the episode with a kind of nostalgic fondness.

At least she'd felt passionately about the person she'd lost her virginity to, and it had been pretty good sex for her first time doing it. Not everyone could say that.

On her return, she found Adam still asleep, his face rumpled and a frown creasing his brow.

'Hey, Adam,' she said gently. 'It's time to get ready for dinner.'

He looked at her through bleary-looking eyes. 'What?'

She shook her head at him. 'This is what you get for drinking so early in the day.'

'Oh, sod off. Leave me alone,' he said, crossly. 'I'm on holiday. I want to catch up on some sleep.'

'Come on. You can sleep later,' she chided, trying to keep the irritation out of her voice. 'Zach's booked a place for us to go for dinner.'

'You go. I'm staying here. I'm not hungry anyway,'

he said, turning away from her and closing his eyes again.

Daisy was unnerved by this turn of events. She didn't know how she felt about going out with Zach on her own.

No, don't be ridiculous.

'Okay, if that's what you want, stay here. I'll go on my own,' she said, and without waiting for Adam's reply, stomped into the bathroom to take a hot, powerful shower.

As the steaming water punished her skin, she tried to clear her mind of all thoughts of Zach and take a moment to reflect on her life. She was in a good position right now. She had a great job, which was very rewarding when everything went well, and she had Adam, who loved her.

But was she truly happy? There always seemed to be something missing, something slightly elusive that she couldn't quite put her finger on. But that was just life, right? It wasn't like it was a game you could complete.

When she returned to the living room of the suite, scrubbed clean and refreshed, she found Adam was fast asleep again.

She'd put on the only dressy skirt that she'd brought, which stopped just above her knees, and paired it with a sleeveless, silk, chemise-style vest. After adding some mascara to her lashes and a slick of dark-pink lipstick to her lips, she felt ready.

She was satisfied with the way she looked, even if it wouldn't compete with the designer couture she was sure to be surrounded by. But she looked dressed enough to be out in Cannes. Elegant, but grounded.

There was a knock on the door as she applied one final coat of lipstick and she tripped over to it in her low-heeled sandals, swinging it open to reveal Zach, his tall frame filling the doorway.

He was dressed in dark, baggy cargo trousers which elongated his legs and a soft, light-blue, cashmere, V-neck jumper which fitted his broad torso perfectly.

Daisy felt the breath leave her body as she gazed at him. He really was heavenly to look at. No wonder he constantly won polls for *sexiest man alive* in the plethora of magazines that loved to feature him.

'Daisy, you look gorgeous as always,' he said, dipping his head in appreciation.

'Looking pretty good yourself,' she replied, hoping the slight squeak in her voice didn't give away just *how* pretty she found him.

'Is Adam ready?' he asked, looking past her into the room.

'He's not coming,' she said, fighting a flush of embarrassment. 'He's sleeping off his hangover.' She was trying hard to keep the annoyance out of her voice, but Zach obviously noticed it.

'Oh,' he said, looking surprised, then a little worried. 'Okay.'

'You don't mind, do you?' she asked hurriedly, suddenly wondering if he'd rather not go out with only her and wait for Adam to be in a better mood for a meal another night.

'No, of course not,' he said, to her relief. 'That is, if you don't mind?' He said this gently, acknowledging the awkwardness that had been between them for so long.

'I don't. So, let's go. I'm starving,' Daisy said confidently, ushering him out and pulling the door closed behind them.

She didn't want to make an issue of this. They would just go for a nice meal, catch up a bit, and then both retire to their respective hotel rooms so they were fresh for the next day.

'Oh, I forgot to say,' Zach said, stopping suddenly, 'you'll need your passport.'

Daisy looked at him in confusion. 'What do you

mean? Where on earth are you taking me?' she asked, floored by this unexpected request.

'Don't worry, I'm not going to sweep you away to some secluded island in the Mediterranean for the night,' he teased. 'You just need it for later, that's all. It's a surprise,' he finished, mysteriously, wagging his eyebrows.

'Ok-aay,' Daisy said slowly, trying not to laugh at the expression on his face and totally failing.

Returning to the room, she grabbed her passport from the safe.

Adam was snoring away on the sofa now and she swept past him, slamming the door behind her, ungraciously hoping it would jolt him out of his drunken stupor.

'Here it is,' she said, waving it at Zach as she caught him up, where he was waiting for the lift.

'Great,' he said, clearly refusing to elaborate on its necessity.

Daisy was intrigued. What could she possibly need it for? She could come up with no reasonable explanation.

I guess I'll just have to wait and see.

The lift doors opened and they both walked in.

* * *

Once they'd exited through the hotel's reception – Zach nodding to a number of people who called out to him on the way – they walked out to the driveway to find a dark-grey Aston Martin DB9 waiting for them, that a valet had pulled around to the front of the hotel.

'Whoa, Zach, you really are doing well for yourself,' Daisy breathed as she took in the sleek interior and snuggled back into the comfortable seat.

'Sadly, it's just a rental,' he admitted ruefully, 'but I was thinking of getting one,' he added, flashing her a wicked grin.

A low pulse began to beat, deep in her body, and she quickly turned away from him to look out of the window as the trees on the Croisette flashed by.

* * *

The restaurant that Zach had chosen was indeed off the beaten track. It was located down a narrow back street and Zach pulled the car over alongside a high brick wall and turned off the engine.

'Right, I know it looks a bit dodgy, but believe me, the food is out of this world,' he promised, smiling confidently at her.

He leapt out of the car and before she had time

to unbuckle her belt, he'd opened her door, proffering his hand.

'Mademoiselle,' he said with aplomb.

Daisy couldn't help but smile. She stretched out her hand and took his, relying on his strength for support as she drew herself up from the low-slung chassis.

'Arm?' he asked her, his eyebrows raised in a mock over-politeness.

'I think I can walk on my own, thanks. I promise not to trip over,' she replied giving him a faux reproving look back.

He laughed and motioned in the direction they needed to go.

The restaurant was dimly lit inside and it took Daisy's eyes a few moments to adjust. Despite its secluded location, it was packed; every table seemed to be filled with loudly chattering French couples, gesturing wildly in their archetypal way.

The maître d' glided over to them. 'Ah, Monsieur Dryden. *Suivez-moi, s'il vous plaît,*' he said, gesturing for them to follow him. He led them to a small table at the back of the restaurant. No one turned to look at them as they moved through the tables, which Daisy found a bit of a relief. She'd been dreading being stared at all night.

Once they were seated, the maître d' sent over their waiter who baffled Daisy with a stream of French, until Zach halted him with a wave of his hand and spoke back in perfect French, apparently placing a drinks order.

'I didn't know you spoke French,' Daisy said, shocked at this new discovery. She'd thought she knew him pretty well, but of course she didn't. There had been a number of intervening years when she'd hardly seen him at all.

'Yeah, I took a course when I was studying at the London Acting Academy and kept going to night classes after that. I thought languages might come in handy one day. I can understand some Spanish too, and a bit of Italian.' He said this with a coy smile, so unlike the over confident Zach that she was used to.

'Right,' was all she could think to say.

This new information felt akin to someone telling her a piece of gossip about her own parents.

'What's wrong?' he asked, apparently concerned by her discomfort.

'Nothing. I just realised I don't really know you that well any more,' she admitted, smiling and shaking her head to dispel his worry.

'No, I guess not,' he agreed. 'I don't think we've ever really sat down and talked. Just you and me.

We've always been surrounded by your and Adam's family. And Adam, of course,' he added quietly.

This hung in the air between them.

They were saved from any further awkwardness by the waiter returning with their drinks.

'I hope you don't mind, I ordered you a champagne cocktail,' Zach said. 'I'm so used to ordering for dinner companions back home, I did it without thinking.'

'No... well... I guess that's okay. Just this once,' Daisy said, not wanting him to think he should do that for her every time. 'It's a good choice for me.'

She loved champagne cocktails, but never would have dared ordering one for herself, especially in a place like this.

Truthfully, she was a little taken aback by Zach's assertive manner. She was so used to Adam asking for her opinion on every little thing that, honestly, it felt good to be looked after like this for a change.

The waiter returned then with two menus.

'So,' Zach said, 'what do you fancy eating? They do great steak frites in here. Or would you prefer something a bit fancier? Have whatever you want. My treat.'

'Well, in that case...' Daisy said, looking down the menu that the waiter had left on the table for her. She carefully considered all the meals on offer, but the thought of steak frites had captivated her and she knew nothing else she chose would compare to it now.

'Steak frites it is,' she said.

He grinned and shifted in his seat, as if pleased that he'd called it right for her again.

Daisy was suddenly hyper aware of his legs under the table only inches away from hers. If she just moved her knee forward very slightly, it would brush against his. She quickly banished the thought, reprimanding herself for letting her mind wander in this direction.

It had to be the alcohol she told herself, deciding to stop drinking until she had some food inside her.

Who knew what she might end up saying if she was drunk?

He, on the other hand, appeared to be drinking sparkling water, she noticed.

'Are you teetotal now?' she asked.

Perhaps he'd had a drink problem that she didn't know about.

Zach laughed. 'No, I'm driving, remember?'

She felt stupid now at her question and her face heated with embarrassment.

'I've got something fun planned for after the

meal,' he added, obviously aware of her discomfort and determined to pull her out of it.

Her passport, which was nestled safely in her bag, flashed into her mind and she wondered again what she could possibly need it for.

'So, you're really not going to tell me why I need a passport tonight?' she probed.

But Zach just shook his head, flashing her a teasing smile.

Despite herself, she laughed, suddenly feeling elated. She was here, in Cannes, reconciled with a good friend that she really cared about, a friend who obviously valued her friendship, in a great restaurant, drinking champagne cocktails and about to go off on an adventure.

She realised with a shock that she hadn't felt excited like this for an awfully long time.

The waiter arrived back at their table and Zach ordered steak frites as well, but rare, while Daisy asked for hers medium rare; normally, she would have said medium to well-done, but she didn't want Zach to think she was unsophisticated.

'I'm just going to powder my nose,' she told him, feeling an urge to be on her own for a few moments to gather her thoughts.

'It's just up the stairs to the left,' he told her, motioning in the direction she needed to go.

'Thanks,' she said, getting up carefully from the table. The cocktail had really gone to her head and she felt a little light headed.

She floated up the stairs and into the ladies' room, stopping on the way to look at her reflection in the mirror. A glowing, happy-looking woman stared back. Her eyes were alight and her skin had tanned a little in the sun, making her whole face radiate health.

I'm okay, she told herself, *I don't need fancy clothes and expensive make-up. I'm an attractive, confident woman. And I'm here with Zach, who a lot of women would be falling over themselves to be with right now.*

At this final thought, she shook her head, trying to dislodge it from her brain. She'd escaped from Zach's presence so she could clear her head for a moment, but it seemed her overactive imagination wasn't going to let her.

After washing her hands and giving herself a hard stare in the mirror, she exited the bathroom and climbed carefully back down the stairs to where Zach was waiting for her, her heart racing more than before she'd left him.

9

When she arrived back at the table, the food had magically appeared.

'That was quick,' she exclaimed, sitting down swiftly so as not to hold up the eating of it any longer. 'Have I really been away that long?'

Zach laughed. 'One of the perks of stardom: getting served before everyone else,' he said with an embarrassed grin.

Daisy shook her head. She still couldn't get used to Zach being famous. It obviously had its upsides, but she couldn't understand how he coped with his every move being documented and gossiped over.

'Do you *like* the fame?' she asked him, tucking

into her delicious-smelling food, unable to wait a moment longer.

'Sometimes,' he said, looking up from his meal that he'd started devouring too, 'but a lot of the time, it's a pain in the arse, to be honest.'

'Yeah, I bet,' she said with a grimace.

'The most brilliant thing is, you can be as boring as you like and people still want to talk to you.'

'God, how sad,' she said, then wrinkled her nose at him when she realised he was only joking.

'Some people really get off on the power of it, though,' he continued. 'There's this one guy,' he paused as if wrestling with himself about whether to continue or not. 'He's been in the business for a long time, but he's only just starting to get notoriety now.' He picked up his drink and took a swig before continuing.

'About a year ago, when I was trying to transition from TV to film, I went for a part that I felt really passionate about. It meant a lot to me – exactly the sort of project I should be getting involved with. It was low budget, but the script was sensational. Anyway, it caused a bit of a stir and my agent pushed for a meeting with the casting director. I met up with her and was desperate to impress her.' He put his cutlery down now, to continue with his tale.

'One of the main characters reminded me of you, as a matter of fact, and I loved the story,' he continued quickly, before Daisy could interject with a question.

'So, I met with this woman, who could have secured me the part. I knew I was perfect for it and so did she. She even said as much. But there was a catch. She suggested that she'd only guarantee me the part if I slept with her.'

Zach paused at this point in the story and looked at her, as if to gauge her reaction to it.

Daisy, who had been feeling increasingly uneasy throughout the telling of the tale, bristled with anger.

'I told her no,' he said forcibly, 'and she turned really fucking cold and told me she'd "get back to me". I knew what that meant, of course. I'd blown it, but for the sake of my professional – and my personal – pride, I couldn't have gone through with it. I wanted to win my parts on pure talent. Anyway, I later found out the actor who got the part agreed to sleep with her. The guy I just mentioned. He was the one who told me, so I know it's true. We have a bit of a rivalry going, which started years back when we found we were always up for the same parts.'

He let out a resentful snort.

'So, he lorded this role he'd won over me. The casting director had apparently told him she didn't think I could hack it in the business and he took pleasure in reminding me of this every time we bumped into each other, which was a lot, unfortunately, as we move in very similar circles. You've probably heard of him. Nathaniel Kingson?'

He looked at her expectantly.

Daisy dredged her memory for the name and came up with a blank. She hadn't had much time for watching films over the last few years; work had been all consuming and she and Adam had preferred to go out for meals with friends if they had any free time, instead of going to the cinema or watching a movie at home.

Throughout his story though, Daisy had felt her anger grow on Zach's behalf. She couldn't believe anyone could be so petty and was proud of Zach for standing up for his principles.

'Yes, I know *of* him. He's awful,' she lied, determined to support him in her renewed role of friend. 'Absolutely no charisma. And you were right not to sleep with that despicable casting director as well. She's giving women with power a bad name,' she finished angrily. 'As if we don't have it hard enough as it is!'

Zach smiled a gracious smile. 'Thanks, Daisy. It means a lot to hear you say that.' He looked at her intently, his eyes searching hers.

Her stomach did an involuntary flip.

'I was really fucking mad with myself for getting into that situation,' he continued, 'even though it was out of my control. And I'm really sorry about this... but I'm afraid it impacted on you too. This all happened just before I came to stay with you and Adam in London. I was in a bad place. I'd lost the part and been made to feel like a fool, Lola was driving me nuts and I knew she was bad news but was finding it really hard to break up with her. And I was really messed up about whether I wanted to stay in a career that was so fickle and soul destroying. I'd had such a positive experience till then and I just felt really... disappointed. That's the thing: when you're doing well, you feel like you can conquer the world, but when things go wrong, it's crushing.'

He swiped an agitated hand through his hair. 'I felt like I was losing control of everything. So, I have another apology to add to the list. I acted like a total shit towards you, and Adam too, and I'm so fucking sorry, Daisy.' His face was a picture of contrition. 'You're one of my oldest friends and I can't stand the thought of losing you. Or Adam,' he added.

Throughout this confession, Daisy felt tears welling in her eyes and she had to fight to stop them spilling over. She cleared her throat. 'It's okay. I forgive you, and so would Adam if he knew why you'd acted that way. Not that he knows about what happened that day between us,' she added, her cheeks heating.

She'd never breathed a word about what had gone on between her and Zach that fateful night, or any of the other times they'd clashed. If that's what you could call it.

Zach was looking at her intently now. His dark features still set in a frown.

'It's okay, Zach, really. Let's just forget it happened, okay?' she said, giving him a smile, which thankfully he returned.

Killer smile, she thought, once again having to force down the fluttering feeling deep in her stomach.

'Do you want any dessert?' he asked. 'Coffee? Another drink?'

'Nothing else for me, thanks. That was perfect.'

'Well, in that case, let's get going,' he said, motioning to the waiter to bring the bill.

After he'd paid for the meal, he had a rapid conversation in French with the maître d', who shook his hand warmly, and they exited into the balmy night air.

'I love the south of France,' Daisy said. 'It's so warm for this time of year here. Why can't it be like this in England? It would make such a difference to my mood if I could sit out under the stars in the evening without shivering my arse off.'

Zach smiled at her. 'You could always move here.'

'You're kidding me, right? Adam would never go for that,' she said, regretting it when his expression appeared to darken for a moment.

Or had she just imagined it?

They clambered back into the car and Zach drove east towards the autoroute.

'So, when are you going to tell me where we're going?' Daisy ventured, looking over at his shadowed profile as he drove.

'I'm not,' he replied, an enigmatic smile on his lips. 'You're just going to have to wait and see.'

'Hmph,' Daisy said in mock annoyance, causing Zach to laugh.

'Want to listen to some music?' he asked, turning on the sound system on the dash in front of him.

'Sure. As long as it's not that appalling techno you used to listen to,' she added.

'Okay then, as it's you, no banging techno,' he agreed. He tossed her his mobile phone and she connected it, choosing a playlist at random, then settled back and let the music wash over her as the night-darkened scenery alongside the autoroute flashed by.

They listened in companionable silence for a while, Daisy thinking about how strange it was to be here with him, not arguing or angry with him for a change. Perhaps they *could* just be friends. As long as she was able to keep her attraction to him in check.

He was doing a good job of keeping her at arm's length too.

Perhaps they'd finally found a comfortable balance between them and this was the beginning of a newfound, happily platonic relationship.

10

After about thirty minutes on the road, Zach signalled to pull off the autoroute and drove under a big sign announcing their destination.

Monaco.

'What are we doing here?' Daisy asked, turning to him in amazement.

'Will you just have some patience, Dizzy!' he admonished her, but smiled wickedly at her obvious delight.

He drove on, following the main route through the city. The road was quiet by now as it was late and he was able to put his foot down. As they swept past large, elegant buildings and down towards Monte Carlo and the harbour, Daisy had a sudden feeling of déjà vu. She knew she'd never been here before but it all seemed so familiar. Then it struck her; they were driving round the Monaco Grand Prix circuit. Whilst at university, one of her housemates had been mad keen on a computer game that had emulated all the grand prix circuits around the world, allowing the player to virtually drive their car around the tracks. She'd been submitted to this game on a regular basis and so was *au fait* with all of them.

'Oh my God!'

'Recognise it?' he asked.

'I do,' she said, 'how brilliant!'

'Wahoo!' they both shouted as they raced through the tunnel, the strip-lights flashing above them, briefly turning to smile at each other in delight, the light throwing wild shadows across their faces.

As the car exited the tunnel, the magnificent vista of the seafront was revealed in all its glory, the water sparkling in the moonlight and huge yachts bobbing gently in the harbour.

Zach turned the car off the road and they drove up a shallow hill, passing beautifully constructed, ancient-looking buildings. As they mounted the brow, then began to descend, Daisy saw a magnificent building rising before them. Its grand, turreted façade gleamed brightly under the spotlights trained on it and a large drive swept around a lush, green island of grass bordered by jazzily coloured flowers.

Zach pulled the car into a parking space next to a red Ferrari and walked swiftly around to open her door for her.

'I could get used to this,' she joked.

Zach smiled back, but she caught a flash of something else in his expression too. What was it? She couldn't quite place it.

'I think I'm having a James Bond moment,' she said, ignoring her concerns.

'Why yesh, Mish Moneypenny,' Zach replied.

'Is that your best Sean Connery impression?' she teased. 'Call yourself an actor?'

He raised his eyebrows at her in affront. 'Give me a break,' he said. 'I usually work with a voice coach for weeks before performing an accent. I know it's not one of my strengths,' he continued before she could interrupt with more teasing, 'but I have a lot of other talents.'

He raised his eyebrow suggestively at her again when he said this, sending heat rushing straight down her spine.

'Good job,' she countered dryly, deliberately ignoring his provocative taunt.

He was not making this *just-being-friends* thing easy for her.

'Come on,' he commanded, touching her arm and motioning for her to walk with him towards the exit.

Her arm tingled where his hand had brushed her skin.

They walked past a row of very expensive-looking classic cars, which were lined up along the drive.

'Wow,' Daisy said, 'look at all those beauties.' Their bodywork gleamed in the light thrown back from the casino's spot-lit frontage.

'Yeah, I know,' Zach said. 'I think the casino owns some of them, but a lot of money definitely flows through this place.'

He ushered her through the doors of the main entrance.

'Passport,' he commanded, holding out his hand to her. She rummaged in her bag and handed it to him. He passed it, along with his, to the lady at the grand front desk who wrote down their details before inviting them to go into the main room of the casino.

It was an incredible sight. The room must have been a ballroom at one point and its towering walls and pale, corniced ceiling gave it real grandeur. Roulette and blackjack tables were set up at intervals along the floor and a magnificent chandelier hung from the ceiling, casting a luminous glow over the proceedings.

The room was thronged with elegantly dressed players, all wearing either evening gowns or dinner jackets.

Daisy suddenly felt completely out of place in her casual outfit.

'Zach, we shouldn't be in here, not dressed like this,' she muttered to him, gesturing to her clothes in dismay. 'Everyone's staring at us,' she added, suddenly aware that they were causing quite a stir among the onlookers. 'God, I'm so not prepared for this holiday,' she said, in a bit of a flap now, her face hot with embarrassment. 'I don't own any designer clothes. I'm going to look like a joke at your film's premiere.'

'Daisy, don't worry about it. They're not looking at us because of what we're wearing,' Zach said. 'It's because they're wondering who the beautiful woman is, with that lucky bastard, Zach Dryden.' He gave her a slow wink.

Daisy could only laugh at that, which helped her relax a little. Though the word 'beautiful' caught in her mind and made her cheeks even hotter.

'Yeah, if you say so,' she agreed, welcoming the distraction from her feelings of inadequacy.

'Daisy, you would look gorgeous wearing a cloth sack,' he stated in his no-nonsense way. 'Now, come on, let's get ourselves some chips.'

He marched over to the cashier and took his phone out, ready to use it to buy the counters they needed to play on the tables.

Daisy hung back, frustrated by her lack of funds available for this kind of fun.

He returned a minute later, proffering her half of his stack of chips.

'What?' she said, in confusion. 'Zach, I don't mean to be a party pooper, but I can't afford to gamble any money at the moment, and I can't afford to pay you back,' she admitted. Shame flooded through her as she thought about her poor status, especially compared to his.

He frowned at her discomfort. 'Daisy, the last thing I wanted was for you to bankrupt yourself coming here. I wanted you and Adam to celebrate with me, like you let me celebrate with you at Andy and Sally's anniversary weekend and on your family holidays. I have more money than I need and I don't have anyone else to share these experiences with. It means a lot to me that you've both come to support me and I want you to have fun while you're here.' He took her hand and gently prised open her fingers, placing the chips into her palm, then closing her fingers back around them.

Daisy looked down at what he'd given her. It was a stack of one-hundred euro chips, probably about a thousand euros in all.

'I can't take this much from you! What if I lose it all?' she gasped.

'Don't worry about it, I've got more money than sh-ense.' He raised an eyebrow at her, cementing the James Bond joke.

'No, seriously Zach, I can't gamble with your money.'

He let out a huff of irritation. 'Daisy, look, I want to enjoy the money I've earnt and I can't think of a better way than watching you lose it at roulette,' he teased. 'Anyway, you used to give me some of your money when we played the slot machines on holiday, when we were kids. I wouldn't have been able to join in otherwise. This is me paying you back for that kindness.'

'That was only the odd pound, here and there,' she argued.

'Well, I'm paying it back – with interest. Please let me?'

Clearly, he wasn't going to give up on persuading her to take it. He seemed to be needing to correct some perceived imbalance he felt.

'Well, if you're sure,' she said, hesitantly.

'Come on,' he said, already walking away, 'there's some space at that table over there.'

He led her over to the roulette table and started to place chips on the board.

It had been a long time since Daisy had played roulette; even then, it had only been a pretend casino at one of her student balls at university, so she was cautious at first and just put one chip down at a time. After winning a bit and losing a bit, she gained some confidence and started putting more and more chips down each time. Zach was liberally covering the board with his own chips now and seemed to be losing rather a lot more than he was winning.

When she pointed this out, he just shrugged and said, 'I guess it's not my lucky day.'

Daisy wasn't sure how to feel about this; she worked damn hard for her money and valued every penny, but it was up to him, she reminded herself. He was a grown up and could make his own choices.

After a happy hour of playing, Zach drew her to one side.

'So, how much are you up?' he asked, motioning towards the chips in her hand.

'Oh, about 800 euros,' she said, checking the stack of chips and feeling a warm buzz about actually winning.

'Okay, well, I could do with a drink. Let's put all our chips on one number, just for the hell of it. You choose it, since you seem to be doing so well,' he suggested.

'What? Really?' she asked. 'Are you sure?' She felt feverish at the thought of it.

'Totally sure,' he said, passing his chips to her.

There were only three left in his stack, but one of them she noticed was worth a thousand euros.

'Zach, I think you've made a mistake. You can't possibly want me to put this on too,' she said, trying to hand the thousand-euro chip back to him.

'Yes, I do. Go on, be brave,' he said, breaking out his devastating smile.

She couldn't refuse him, not when he looked at her like that.

Going back to the table, she put all the chips on number seventeen, with a shaky hand.

They watched with bated breath as the roulette wheel was spun and the small ball bounced its way round the numbers.

Daisy's heart thumped like crazy in her chest and she could barely look, but as the wheel slowed down, she stared in incredulity at where it finally rested.

At number seventeen.

She gasped, her hands flying to her mouth in shock and turned to find Zach staring at her, a look of absolute amazement on his face.

'Wahoo!' they both shouted together for the second time that evening, laughing uproariously and slapping their hands together in a high five. Zach grabbed hold of her round the waist and lifted her up against his body, hugging her to him. He twirled her around until she felt dizzy, finally stopping and pulling his head back to look her directly in the eyes, which were still on his level.

She was suddenly conscious of his heart beating against her chest, mirroring the rapid pounding of blood through her body. Her nerve endings felt like they were on fire and her breath was shallow and heavy in her chest.

They stared at each other, their faces only inches apart.

Daisy's lips tingled in anticipation of what might come next – was he going to kiss her? – but Zach gently placed her back down on the floor and drew away from her.

'Well, that was unexpected,' he muttered, running his hand over his thick, dark hair. 'Let's go and collect our winnings.'

But Daisy, flushed with the excitement of winning and unwilling to break the amazing connection they'd forged between them in experiencing it together, paused before saying, 'Wait. Let's just have one more game.' She looked at him beseechingly, desperate to keep this happy feeling alive.

'Don't be an idiot, Dizzy,' he said, gently, cuffing her shoulder in a brotherly manner. 'You have to quit while you're ahead.'

Disappointment surged through her. She so badly wanted this feeling to go on and she was worried that the new closeness between them would be broken as soon as they left the table.

On the other hand, she was irked by his ability to make her feel like she was being a naïve kid, which brought back memories of all the times in their past when he'd derided her for her choices.

'Just because you've not had a lucky streak tonight doesn't mean I shouldn't pursue mine,' she said defensively.

'Daisy,' he said quietly, but with command in his voice, 'come away with me now or I'm going to put you over my shoulder and carry you away kicking and screaming in front of all these lovely people. For your own good.'

The teasing humour in his voice brought her up short and she checked herself. She *was* being an idiot; he was quite right. She should be happy with what they'd achieved and take a break.

She wondered suddenly if she'd got him wrong when he'd teased her as kids. His manner had made her feel demeaned and berated, but perhaps it was just his misguided way of trying to find humour in a situation. Perhaps in her innocence, she'd misread his sarcastic, cutting comments and not recognised he was actually joking with her.

Well, from now on, she wasn't going to take any of them seriously, she told herself, pleased by this epiphany.

'O-kay,' she sighed, in mock annoyance, slapping him gently on the arm. 'But only because I don't want you hurting your back before your big night.'

She grinned up at him and he snorted back,

looking as if he wanted to say something else, but stopping himself.

'Right,' he said after a short pause, 'where's the bar?' He looked around and spotted it, heading towards it before Daisy could ask him what was on his mind.

Zach had already reached the counter when she caught him up, and was ordering himself a soft drink.

'What can I get you?' he asked.

'I'll have a glass of champagne,' she said confidently. Now she was on such a high, she wanted to keep buzzing. Zach ordered her drink and paid the tab when the bartender brought them over.

'Let's find a seat,' he said, starting to move through the tables. Daisy watched him go, his statuesque figure causing a stir amongst the other customers in the bar. Women turned to stare at him as he passed by, appreciatively glancing up and down at his athletic physique. Daisy remembered the pub in Fowey and how much of an effect he'd had even then, before he'd become famous. *And look at us now*, she thought to herself. *So much water under the bridge. So many tears in the shower.*

She followed the path he'd taken, aware of the interested stares she was provoking from the seated women, who'd just watched Zach go by with such fascination. Luckily, he'd found a table in the corner and put his drink down on it and she joined him there a moment later, pulling out one of the chairs and flopping down onto it with a relieved sigh.

'I'm just going to cash in our chips,' he said, proffering his hand for hers.

She relinquished them unwillingly. She'd got used to their comforting weight in her hand.

Oh well, maybe one day I'll come back and win some of my own money.

Her thoughts flicked to her disastrous holiday clothes, now wishing she'd had the guts to gamble with her own money. She would have been able to buy herself a whole new wardrobe with her winnings if she'd been brave enough. Sipping her drink pensively, she waited for Zach to return. He came striding back a few minutes later and without explanation handed her a wad of cash.

'What's this?' she asked in confusion, noticing that he'd given her what must have amounted to thousands of euros.

'Your cut of the winnings,' he said nonchalantly.

'But—' she began, but he waved his hand, cutting off further speech from her.

'You won it fair and square. It's yours. Anyway,

you just won me a cool hundred thousand euros. I
can afford that DB9 now,' he said with a wink. 'Buy
yourself something fun and frivolous,' he added.

Her breath seemed to be caught in her chest.
'Zach, I can't take this. It's yours,' she protested.

But he shook his head and looked deliberately
away, crossing his arms and closing the subject.
Daisy thought about it for a second. He'd loaned her
the money to play with. She'd won the proceeds off
it with her own luck though, so why shouldn't she
keep it? He'd not lost anything. In fact, she'd won
him back any money he'd lost – and then some – by
picking number seventeen on the wheel. *Yes, okay*,
she decided, a thrill of excitement rising through
her*, the hell with it, I will keep it*. With a resolute nod
in his direction, she put the cash into her bag.

'Thank you,' she said, with feeling.

Zach just shrugged, the corner of his mouth tug-
ging into a satisfied smile.

'You were just telling me how you hated all your
clothes. Now you can get some new ones.' He raised
his hand, finger pointing up in a *just a moment* gesture. 'Actually, let me ask my PA to close a store for
us tomorrow and you can go and shop for a new
dress for the premiere in peace. If I drop my name,

I'm sure I can get them to lend you a designer gown for the evening so you can spend your money on some stuff that you'll actually wear again. What do you say? We could get Adam a tux at the same time?' he added.

'Oh!' Daisy said, completely taken aback by this suggestion. She'd never even dreamed she'd be in the position to have an entire store closed just for her. *What a rush!*

Well, she may as well make the most of it. It wasn't as if she got offers like this every day.

'That would be fantastic,' she breathed, smiling in disbelief at his thoughtfulness.

'Fine. Consider it done. I'll come and pick you both up about eleven tomorrow then,' he said.

'Okay,' she agreed, elation surging through her. It was *so nice* to be looked after like this.

She realised with a shock that she'd hardly thought about Adam all evening and the elation gave way to shame. But it was his own fault. If he hadn't been in such a nihilistic mood...

'Daisy?' Zach said, gently, breaking into her thoughts.

'Hmm?'

'I've got something for you,' he said, drawing a

small, black case out of one of the side pockets of his cargo trousers.

Daisy stared at it, curiosity making her heart race.

'What is it?' she asked, taking it out of his proffered hand.

'Open it and see,' he said, looking at her intently.

She gave him a searchingly look, before flipping the lid open. It was a small, platinum pendant in the shape of a knot with a diamond buried in the centre of it, hanging from a delicately spun chain. The stone caught the light as she held it up and bright prisms flashed into her eyes.

'It's beautiful,' she gasped, looking over at his expectant face. 'But why on earth would you buy me this?' she asked.

'It's a gift to say sorry for the way I treated you.' He leaned forward in his chair towards her and she caught a waft of his delicious scent in the air. 'To show how much I value your and Adam's friendship. You're the closest thing I have to family and I wanted you to know how much I care about you both,' he said, his face a picture of sincerity.

'Zach, you didn't need to do this. I acted just as badly as you did, so you really don't have anything to apologise for.'

'Please take it, though. It would mean a lot to me if you'd accept it. It's a friendship knot. Hopefully, you'll think of me occasionally when you wear it,' he added.

Daisy was overwhelmed. She'd never owned anything so beautiful.

'Okay. Well, thank you,' she said with feeling. There was a loaded pause where they just looked at each other. 'I hope you didn't get one of these for Adam as well. I don't think he's got any outfits he can wear a diamond pendant with.' She smiled at her own joke but was disturbed to see he wasn't smiling back.

'I got him something different,' he said, patting the pocket on the other side of his cargo trousers. 'Some cufflinks. I was hoping I could spend some time with him, just him and me, while we're all here. I think he's still pissed off with me, judging by his performance earlier,' he said, a flash of hurt crossing his face.

'Don't worry about him,' Daisy reassured him, flapping a hand. 'He's just being a facetious arse at the moment. I don't know why. Stressed from over-work, probably. He'll be fine tomorrow.'

Zach half grinned at this. 'He always was a mercurial bastard,' he said, nodding slowly.

Except he wasn't. Not really. He was always pretty straightforward and reliable when it came to how he felt about things and how he acted. At least he was with her.

'Yeah,' Daisy said, choosing not to argue and let it go. Perhaps Zach had a different experience with him. She stifled a yawn, feeling tiredness wash through her. She'd been up early that morning after all, ready to catch the flight to Nice, and it had to be well into the early hours by now.

Zach noticed her sudden droop and took the case with the necklace out of her hand.

'Come here. I just want to see this on you, then we'll get going,' he said, picking the fine chain up and undoing the delicate clasp.

Daisy leaned towards him and Zach put his arms around her neck, drawing her closer so that he could close the clasp around the tiny loop. The close proximity of his body caused a gentle shiver to run thorough her, and she drank in his scent, closing her eyes in appreciation.

He drew back and looked at her admiringly.

'It suits you,' he said, clearly pleased with his choice of present for her. 'Come on, we'd better get you back or you're going to be too tired to enjoy spending your winnings on all those beautiful clothes.'

'Oh, I'll never be too tired for that,' she said, but stifled another yawn.

He grinned.

'I just have to nip to the ladies. I'll meet you in the entrance lobby,' she told him, draining the remainder of her drink and rising from the table before setting off towards the toilets.

After using the elegant facilities, she checked her appearance before leaving. She was starting to look tired now, but her skin still glowed with happiness. The necklace gleamed around her neck and she touched it gently, admiring the beautiful shape of it.

As she exited the bathroom and walked to the entrance lobby, she saw Zach by the doors, waiting for her.

Except he wasn't alone.

A slim, elegantly dressed woman was leaning in towards him, their bodies almost touching. She was talking intently, her attention entirely focused on him.

He glanced away in Daisy's direction and she saw a flash of entreaty on his face as their eyes met.

Relief washed over her as she realised he was

uncomfortable in this woman's company and wanted to escape from her.

She made up her mind about what to do in a flash and marched confidently over to him, sliding one arm around his waist and bringing her other hand up to cup his jaw and drawn his head down so she could place a firm kiss on his lips.

She luxuriated in the feeling of his mouth against hers for just those two seconds, before drawing slowly away from him.

'Come on, darling. It's time for me to take you home and ravish you,' she breathed as huskily as she could manage, looking deep into his eyes.

He stared back at her, his pupils blown, and she could have sworn she heard his breath hitch in his throat.

The woman took a step away from them and when Daisy turned to look at her, she could see from her expression that she knew she'd been given her marching orders. Raising her hand in a wave of goodbye, she glided away from them.

Daisy's lips were still tingling from their connection with Zach's and turning back to him, she saw incredulity written across his face.

'Sorry,' she said, finding she didn't mean it one bit. 'I didn't know what else to do. She looked like the type who needed to see a clear public display of affection to get the message.'

'Not a problem,' he replied, rubbing his hand over his jaw, then reaching out to pull her against his body in a friendly bear hug. 'Feel free to save me any day,' he said, into her hair. She felt so safe there, pressed against his body.

To her disappointment, he immediately released her. 'Come on. We'd better get back on the road.'

She walked out with him, her insides jumbled.

Without another word, they got into the car and set off back to Cannes.

Despite her tiredness, Daisy didn't want the night to end. Zach had put some tunes on again and she relaxed back into the uber-comfy seat, letting the music soothe her.

They spent the rest of the journey in silence, Daisy growing steadily sleepier from the lulling effects of the drive and by the time Zach pulled into the Carlton's forecourt, she was nearly asleep.

'Hey, Diz, we're back,' he murmured, rousing her out of her stupor.

She stretched, then yawned into her hand, nodding. 'Okay, great.' Turning to look at him sitting there in the semi-darkness, her stomach swooped at the expression on his face. He was staring at her intently, as if he was thinking about kissing her.

Or was that her overactive imagination playing tricks on her again?

Oh Lord.

Her heart was racing again and her skin tingled all over, like all the hair on her body had stood up at once. She needed to get out of there. Right now. Before she gave in to the intense urge to say or do something she shouldn't.

'I'll see you in reception at eleven,' she muttered, reaching for the handle before he could reply.

'Sure,' she heard him say, in his low, gravelly voice behind her, as she scrambled out of the car. 'Night.'

Not looking back, she walked quickly through the hotel's reception and straight into the lift that was fortuitously waiting there for her.

As it made its smooth journey upwards, she allowed herself to reflect on the events of the night. She'd probably had the most fun she'd ever had in her entire life tonight. This thought produced a pang of something like guilt – because Adam hadn't been a part of it – which she quickly banished. It had been his decision not to come, after all.

Back in the suite, she found Adam had crawled

into bed and flung all her neatly laid-out clothes onto the floor in a heap.

Sighing in annoyance, she picked them up and laid them carefully on the chaise longue at the end of the bed, then went to get washed and undressed, before climbing in next to him, preparing herself for a disturbed night as a loud, shuddering snore came from his direction.

11

Daisy awoke groggily the next morning to find that Adam was already up and out of bed.

She looked blearily over at her phone on the night stand and was shocked to see that it was already quarter past ten. She was supposed to be meeting Zach in the lobby in forty-five minutes and she really needed a shower and some breakfast before setting out on their promised shopping trip.

'Adam?' she shouted, jumping out of bed and desperately searching around for one of the complimentary bathrobes.

Adam appeared from the adjoining room and watched her hunting for the errant piece of clothing, an inquisitive smile on his face.

'Morning, sleepyhead. Good night, was it?' he asked, coming over and pulling her to him. He smelt sour from all the alcohol he'd consumed the previous day.

'Ugh! You stink!' she muttered, without thinking, struggling out of his embrace. Finally managing to locate a dressing gown, she pulled her arms into it and secured it at the waist. 'I mean, yes, it was fun,' she said distractedly, turning to clock the look of hurt on his face.

She didn't have time to soothe him right now, though. She needed to get a move on if she was going to be ready for eleven o'clock.

'Where did you go?' he asked, obviously hurt at her rejection and watching her in consternation as she flapped around the room, choosing an outfit to put on after her shower. All her clothes were creased after Adam's disrespectful handling of them.

'We went for steak frites at some little back street restaurant Zach knows,' she replied, uncomfortably aware of how much work she'd need to do to tone down the events of the previous evening, so as not to make Adam resentful.

She didn't want him to think she'd had more fun without him, even if it was true.

He'd annoyed her with his antics the day before,

sure, but looking at him now, standing there with his hair tousled and all his boyish charm on show, she felt a sting of guilt at her blatant disregard for his well-being the previous night.

No. He was the one who decided to get so drunk he couldn't even manage to go out for dinner.

She didn't need to pander to him; he was a grown up and she wasn't his mother.

'How glamorous,' he muttered, with a sarcastic smirk. 'I would have thought old superstar Zach could have done better than that.' He seemed pleased with his cutting wit.

Daisy's blood started to boil.

'And then he took me to Monaco and we raced around the Grand Prix track before winning thousands of euros at roulette in the casino,' she countered, unable to resist the urge to get back at him for his spiteful tone.

Adam's face fell.

'Huh,' he said, looking suddenly much less pleased with himself. 'I hope you didn't gamble with any of our money?'

Daisy sighed in exasperation and shook her head at him. 'No, Adam, I didn't. We played with Zach's money. We don't even have any money in our joint account at the moment,' she added, only just managing to control the annoyance in her voice. 'Anyway, we don't have time for arguing this morning. Zach's meeting us in the hotel lobby at eleven. He's closing a store for us so we can go shopping for clothes for his film's premiere,' she added, willing him to respond positively to this announcement.

Unfortunately, it was not to be.

'Shopping!' he said crossly. 'I'm not spending my precious holiday time in some nobby shop trying on bloody *clothes*.'

'Adam, we need to get you a dinner jacket for the premiere and party tonight. It's black tie, apparently,' she said, unable to keep her exasperation with him out of her voice.

'Daisy, no,' he stated vehemently. 'I brought my suit. That's going to have to do.'

'Argh!' she shouted in frustration. 'Listen, why don't I just pick you one up then? You go and do whatever it is you want to do this morning and I'll meet you somewhere for lunch? How about the Petite Majestic? Someone at work told me that's supposed to be great,' she said hopefully.

She was worried now that he'd foil her much-anticipated morning of fun, shopping and feeling special. Not to mention being able to use the experience to add colour to her report for Flash.

'How on earth are you going to afford to buy new designer clothes?' he asked crossly. 'You were complaining only the other day about how little savings you have at the moment.'

Daisy paused for a moment, weighing up her options. Should she admit that Zach had given her the money that she was desperately excited about spending? She knew this would make Adam angry, but what the hell, he was already in a rotten mood, she may as well be entirely honest and take the insults he was bound to throw at her. Get it all over and done with in one go.

'I won some last night on the roulette table,' she said, after a beat.

'I thought you said you were playing with Zach's money?' he said, a frown now marring his features.

'I was. He gave me some of the winnings,' she said, bracing herself for the angry onslaught that she knew was coming. Adam was nothing if not proud about money and he hated to be in debt to anyone.

'Daisy, you can't seriously be thinking of accepting money from Zach,' he said, his voice shaking with anger.

'Look, I've already taken it. I won it fair and square. Zach pretty much lost all his but still managed to come out on top because of me.'

'Lucky old Zach,' Adam said dryly, his eyes narrowed in petty annoyance.

'I'm not discussing it any more,' she said, ignoring him. 'I'm buying myself some well-deserved clothes and that's that.' She swept out of the room and into the bathroom before he could say another word.

She took a quick hot shower, scrubbing herself hard in her fury. Adam could wind her up so badly sometimes, she thought, now drying herself furiously.

By the time she walked back into the bedroom, she'd started to calm down and hurriedly dressed, grabbing a pair of khaki shorts and a red, short-sleeved, vintage t-shirt with a coat of arms logo blazoned across the front.

Adam was in the adjoining living area, staring angrily at the television, which was showing an advert for a French supermarket.

She stuffed her feet into her sandals and approached the sofa where he was sitting.

'Adam?' she said gently, willing him to respond reasonably.

'Yeah,' he replied, not looking at her.

'Are you sure you don't want to come?'

'Yes, I'm sure,' he replied huffily. 'I thought *we*

could spend a bit of time together this morning, that's all. I feel like I haven't seen you properly for months and I was looking forward to bit of us time. You know?' he asked pleadingly.

Daisy experienced a wave of shame.

He was right, they hadn't had much time on their own recently, but she was desperately sad at the thought of not going on the exclusive shopping trip now. She'd probably never get an opportunity like this again and she'd have plenty of time to make it up to Adam afterwards.

'Please, Adam. I really want to go. I won't enjoy myself later if I feel uncomfortable in my outfit. I won't be long, I promise.' She held up both palms in a pleading gesture. 'I'll meet you for lunch at one o'clock at the Petite Majestic, okay?' she said, her body tense, willing him to respond favourably.

She saw his shoulders drop in defeat. 'Okay then. Go. I'll see you later,' he mumbled. 'Don't be late,' he added unnecessarily.

She was very rarely late for anything and he knew it.

'Thank you,' she said, gratefully. 'I'll get you a dinner jacket at the same time. See you later.' Glancing at her watch, she saw it was already eleven o'clock. Breakfast would have to wait, even though her stomach was grumbling in protest.

She raced to the lift, which luckily descended straight to the lobby.

Zach was already waiting for her, sitting in a chair, his broad back to the middle of the room and his mobile in his hand, which he appeared to be reading something on. He looked up as she approached.

'Aha! There you are,' he said. 'No Adam? He's not drunk again?' he asked in jest.

'No,' she said, unable to raise a grin. 'He refused to come shopping. Not his scene, apparently.'

'Fair enough,' Zach said, though a slight frown crossed his face. 'Well, in that case, let's go.'

He rose gracefully from the chair, putting his phone in his back pocket, and escorted her out.

Outside, he walked straight to a car that was waiting for them by the doors and motioned for her to get in.

As she clambered inside, she could hear people start to shout Zach's name and he hurriedly shut the door on them and directed the driver to move away quickly. The windows were tinted so they could see out, but no-one could see in, and Daisy was unnerved to see a crowd of people trying to peer into the car, feeling grateful for the privacy the blacked-out windows afforded.

'How are you feeling today?' Zach asked. 'Not too tired from our adventure last night, I hope?'

'I'm fine, thanks,' she replied. 'I slept like a log. I've only just woken up as a matter of fact.'

'Lucky you,' he said, with a raised eyebrow. 'I've been up since six, giving interviews.' He yawned after he said this and she noticed now that he had dark circles around his eyes.

'I had no idea you had to get up that early this morning. We shouldn't have stayed out so late.'

Guilt trickled through her. He was here working after all. In her excitement last night, she'd forgotten that.

'Don't worry about it,' he said, brushing her apology away. 'I'm used to it. It was a great night. I wouldn't have missed it for the world.' He looked over and smiled his devastating smile at her. Daisy felt her insides melt. She suddenly longed to be able to pull him to her and hug him, but she knew that would be a terrible idea. He'd been very careful not to be too tactile with her since they'd met again this time and she didn't want to risk their newly re-founded friendship by letting her heart rule her head.

And she had Adam's feelings to consider.

'So, I've arranged for one of the designer shops to close for an hour for us,' Zach said, breaking into her thoughts. 'I asked my PA to find somewhere that might suit your style. Elegant, but not overly fussy and a little bit quirky.'

'Great,' she replied, taken aback by his perceptiveness. 'Sounds wonderful.'

Zach nodded in appreciation of her pleasure.

They soon pulled up outside one of the designer stores on the main shopping street and the driver walked round to speak to Zach before going into the shop to announce their arrival.

After a minute, the manager of the store came out and introduced herself, shaking first Zach's hand, then hers, warmly and inviting them both into the shop.

All the customers had been ushered out and Daisy experienced a moment of embarrassment at causing them trouble, before shrugging the feeling off. It was about time she let go of her neuroses. She'd worked damned hard recently, without a proper break, and deserved some fun.

* * *

The shop was one of those ones that seemed to have hardly any clothes on the rails.

Daisy walked tentatively over to the nearest rack and started looking through them, feeling like an interloper. This was so different to shopping in the high street chain stores she was used to. The materials the clothes were made from were obviously top quality and she delighted in the feel of them against her fingers. Examining a silky, halter-neck dress, she looked at the price tag and nearly swallowed her tongue.

Good grief.

This was another world she'd walked into.

Feeling a bit nervous now, she turned to locate Zach, who was watching her with an intent look in his eye. The intensity of it made her involuntarily shiver as all the nerves under her skin tingled.

She smiled at him then quickly looked away.

Out of the corner of her eye, she saw him walk over to a seated area near the changing cubicles and sit down, taking out his phone.

She continued to sift through the clothes. There were some beautiful things here. Zach had been spot-on; they were elegant but slightly unusual in design, exactly right for her. The rich colours delighted her and she began to take pieces off the rails to try on. She found a pair of black trousers made from a very soft, heavy material and added them to the pile that was growing in her arms.

One of the shop assistants came over then and gently took the clothes away from her and went to hang them in the changing room, ready for her to try them on. This left her free to grab more things that she liked the look of. There was no way she was going to be able to afford them all, but that didn't mean she couldn't enjoy trying them all on.

There was a delicate pink cashmere jumper with a turtle neck that felt to her like the softest thing she'd ever touched, its subtle colour drawing her to it like a magnet, and she added it to her choices, not daring to check the price tags any more.

When she'd collected a good number of things to try on, she retired to the changing room. Zach was now speaking quietly into his phone and gave her an acknowledging nod as she passed him.

She pulled the curtain across and started to undress, choosing the soft, black trousers and pink jumper to try on first. Once dressed, she admired herself in the mirror. The colour of the jumper looked great against her skin and she luxuriated in the feel of the delicate wool. The trousers fitted her well around the waist and hips too and fell in a gentle line to her knees where they then flared out, lengthening the look of her legs and showing off her curves. She pulled back the curtain to show Zach, who was waiting on the other side.

The look on his face told her that he approved.

'You look great,' he said, nodding at her.

She smiled back appreciatively, then turned and went back into the cubicle to try on the next outfit. The next couple of things she tried on really suited her too, fitting her beautifully. *This is what you're paying for*, she thought to herself, finally checking the price tags and groaning in shock at the amounts they were asking.

'Daisy?' Zach said, from the other side of the curtain.

'Yes?' she called back.

'We might have found a dress for you to wear this evening.'

She adjusted the final top she was trying on and pulled the curtain back to reveal Zach standing there with the manager of the store, a red gown held out in his hand.

It had to be the most beautiful thing Daisy had ever seen.

It was a deep blood red and its delicate material seemed to glow in the soft light of the shop. It was strapless, apart from a single, thin, spaghetti strap which crossed from under one arm across the neckline and over the shoulder to the opposite side on the back. The fine boning on the bodice gave it a structured look and the material flared out from the hips, before pulling gently in at the knees and flaring out again suddenly at the bottom in a short, fish-tail train. Zach turned it round on its hanger to show her the back, which was cut low and finished at the bottom of the cut-out with three tiny heart-shaped buttons.

'It's beautiful,' she whispered. 'Can I really borrow it?' she asked the store manager, who nodded her consent.

'Thank you,' she said with a tremor in her voice. She thought she might burst into tears at a strange rush of emotions that were threatening to overwhelm her. 'Can I try it on?' she asked.

'Of course,' the manager said, nodding curtly.

Zach handed it to her and with a grateful smile at him she strode back into the changing room and pulled the curtain shut.

Just as she was carefully removing her outfit ready to try the dress on, Zach's phone starting ringing. She heard him answer.

'Yeah? What, really? What time?' His voice became fainter as he walked away to take the call in private. She was just undoing the dress to put it on when Zach called to her again through the curtain.

'Daisy? I'm really sorry about this. That was my PA. Apparently, they've scheduled me in for a last-minute interview which starts in about two minutes. I'm going to have to go and leave you to it.'

Disappointment rushed through her. She was having so much fun and she really wanted Zach to see her in the dress. She kept her feelings in check though, not wanting to seem too needy.

'Okay, don't worry, I'll be fine,' she said with as much good humour as she could muster.

'I'll see you later, okay? I've asked my PA to drop off the tickets and directions for the premiere and party afterwards at your hotel. I'll see you there.'

She heard him murmur something to the store manager in French before striding away, the shop door banging closed behind him.

Daisy felt a swell of sadness at his going. How had she ever thought she hated him before? He was kinder and more considerate than she'd ever given him credit for. It just went to show how little she really knew him, even after all these years.

Both of them being older and more sure of themselves had helped too, though. She was definitely able to handle her emotions better now.

Sighing, she carefully dropped the dress over her head, allowing it to slip gently down her body. It felt heavenly to wear. The material clung to her figure in all the right places and the undulating shape gave her the most fantastic curves. The colour was just right on her too. It brought a healthy glow to her cheeks and her dark hair contrasted beautifully with the rich red tone.

After admiring herself for a moment in the mirror, she strode out to the main floor of the shop. The manager was waiting for her and clapped her hands in delight when she saw how well the dress fitted her.

'I 'ave some perfect shoes to go wiz it,' she exclaimed, her pretty French accent sounding like music to Daisy's ears.

She left and went through a staff door, returning a minute later with a pair of beautiful, dark-red shoes. They were made out of soft leather with a sharply pointed toe and tiny straps criss-crossing over where the top of her foot would be. Daisy raised her eyes at the length of the heels though. She'd never worn anything so high before – she'd never needed to, feeling comfortable with her height. In these, she'd be almost as tall as Adam.

She took them from the manager and, sitting down first, put them carefully on her feet. When she stood up, she nearly toppled over on the spindly heels, but managed to steady herself in time. Walking carefully to the nearest mirror and lifting her dress a bit to see them, she admired them in the reflection. They were perfect.

'Unfortunately, I cannot loan zese to you,' the manager said, nodding down at them. 'You would 'ave to purchase them if you want zem.'

Well, she had to have them. The dress was crying out to be worn with them. Maybe she could wear them again one day, if she was ever in the position to own a gown like the one she was wearing. Unlikely, but you never knew. Though perhaps Zach would invite them to another premiere some time and she could hire one like it.

If not, they'd be a wonderful memento from her time here. Or she could sell them. She wasn't sure she'd be able to bring herself to do that, though.

'I'll take them,' she said, turning to the manager and smiling. She walked slowly back to the changing room and undressed, pulling her old clothes back on. She felt dowdy in them now, compared to the magnificence of the dress that she'd just been wearing. With trouble, she chose three of the outfits she'd tried on and loved and took them, together with the shoes and dress to the till. She was shocked to find that all together, they cost nearly all the euros Zach had given her and she handed over the money sadly, telling herself it was money she'd won, so it wasn't really real.

Easy come, easy go.

'You are ver' lucky to have such a wonderful boyfriend, no?' the sales assistant at the counter said in her lulling French accent.

Daisy gave her an awkward smile, her pulse tripping.

A terrible, intangible idea had begun to brew in the back of her mind, which she kept pushing away.

No. She couldn't let it get a hold of her.

None of this was real. It was a Hollywood fairytale.

She needed to pull herself together and go and have lunch with Adam, her actual boyfriend.

Gathering her purchases in their sleek, white, cardboard bags, she thanked the shop's staff and stepped out onto the street, pushing away a slow, sinking feeling of dread as she headed toward the lunch venue – and Adam.

12

The Petite Majestic was located behind the grand Majestic Hotel on a small back street.

It was already busy when Daisy got there, with drinkers spilling out onto the pavement in front of it. She searched around for Adam, but couldn't locate him.

Perhaps he was inside, she thought, heading into the bar.

Nope. No sign of him there either.

She was just about to go outside again when she spotted his fair head leaning over a table tucked into the very corner of the bar. She started to make her way over to him but halted in her tracks when she saw he was sitting there with a woman – a very attractive woman. They seemed to be getting on really well and Daisy felt a sting of annoyance as she watched her touch Adam on the arm in a possessive sort of way. She was smiling into his eyes too and he was responding to her in a very positive manner.

Daisy could tell by his body language that he was deeply attracted to this person and as she watched them, she saw him raise his hand to the woman's face and gently brush something away from her cheek. The woman laughed at this attention and leant into him, their faces barely inches away from each other.

Daisy's gut twisted uncomfortably. Who was she? She'd never seen her before in her life and she was pretty sure she knew everyone that Adam did. He must have met her here in the bar.

She felt a surge of anger at his blatant flirting, but then checked herself. What was she complaining about? If she was being truthful with herself, she was just as bad as him, if not worse. At least he wasn't carrying on with some bizarre pseudo friendship thing with her best friend. Even though nothing had happened with Zach recently, if anyone had seen them together last night, they probably would have assumed they were a couple, just as the shop assistant had.

They'd always had this undeniable mutual attraction that made them react in strange ways towards each other and it was barely being kept in check at the moment.

She backed away from the table slowly, stumbling slightly and knocking into a man who nearly spilt his drink into his lap. Mumbling an apology, she raced out of the bar and down the nearest street. She needed to get away and be on her own to reflect on what she'd just seen and how it was making her feel.

Down another of the innocuous-looking back streets, she came across a small, quiet café and went in, the bell jangling behind her.

She found a table at the back and slumped down into the chair wearily. It was exhausting dealing with all this pent-up emotion.

The waitress came over and she ordered a croque monsieur and a coffee.

She rubbed her eyes and sighed. What was she going to do? Her world was being turned upside down and she felt like she was losing her grip on reality.

If Adam asked her why she'd stood him up, she'd have to tell him she lost track of time and when she'd gone looking for him, she couldn't see him anywhere, so had assumed he'd gone back to the hotel.

Her order arrived quickly and she wolfed it down, suddenly reminded of the breakfast that she'd missed. She was knocking the crumbs off her hands when she became aware of a tall figure looming over her and looked up to find a stunningly handsome man looking down at her. His dark hair, which was lighter at the very ends, as if it had been bleached by the sun – but had to have had help from a hair-dresser – was worn pushed back from his face, she suspected to best show off his expressive, golden-brown eyes. He stared at her with open interest and his striking face broke into a smile as she gazed back up at him.

'Hi there,' he said, in a deep American drawl. 'Have we met somewhere?'

Daisy knew she'd never met him, but there was something familiar about him that she couldn't quite place.

'No, I don't think so,' she replied, smiling politely.

'Mind if I sit down?' he asked, and before she could answer, he'd drawn back the chair opposite her and lowered his fit-as-you-like body down into it.

'Er, no,' she said, somewhat after the fact.

'Great. All the other tables seem to be taken. The

coffee's fantastic in here and it's so quiet. It's really good to get away from the crowds, don't you think?' he asked. His manner was confident, but Daisy found him a little overbearing.

'Hmm,' she agreed, unsure why he'd chosen to sit with her and reluctant to give too much of herself away. There was just something a bit *off* about him.

'So, what's your name?' he asked, looking at her enquiringly.

'Daisy,' she said, not entirely comfortable with telling him, but not sure how avoid it without seeming rude.

'Beautiful name,' he said. 'My friends call me Sonny. I hope you're going to be one of them,' he said, as if he was used to reeling out this line, which, it seemed to Daisy, he probably was. His whole demeanour screamed *player*. 'So, Daisy. What are you doing in Cannes?' he asked, propping his elbows on the table and leaning forwards, making her feel uncomfortable enough to lean back away from him.

'I'm on holiday,' she said. 'A friend invited me to the premiere of his film tonight,' she added, unsure whether she should actually be telling him this. He could be one of those hangers-on that Zach was talking about yesterday.

'Really?' he said, raising his eyebrows. 'That

wouldn't be the premiere for *Damascus Days*, would it?'

'Er, yes,' she confirmed, too shocked by his insight to think of a decent lie to tell him.

'Well, I might bump into you there then. I've been involved with that movie myself. Are you going to the party afterwards?' he asked.

'Uh, yeah... maybe,' she hedged, feeling really uncomfortable under his intense stare now.

He was a stunning-looking man and clearly very charismatic, but there was something about his manner she just didn't like.

'Anyway,' she said. 'I've got to get going. It was great to meet you, Sonny,' she added, rising from the table and making her way over to the cash till to pay for her lunch.

'Sure, it was great to meet you too,' he called after her.

She paid quickly and turned to find he was watching her. A cold shiver ran down her spine at the acquisitive expression on his face. Giving him a hesitant wave, she walked as quickly as she could out of the café, pulling the door firmly shut behind her.

13

Halfway back to the hotel, Daisy suddenly remembered she hadn't picked up a dinner jacket for Adam. She doubled back and took the road that ran past the Hilton towards the centre of the town. She was pretty sure she'd find a dress hire shop down there somewhere. She'd spotted a couple of people earlier coming from that direction with suit carriers draped carefully over their arms.

A few minutes' walk down the road, she came across a place that looked like just the ticket. Going in, she was relieved to see an array of dinner jackets and all the accoutrements laid out on display. After explaining to the salesperson in pidgin French what size of jacket and trousers she needed, she picked out a crisp white dress shirt and pitch-black bow tie to go with them, opting for the ready tied one as she didn't think Adam knew how to tie a bowtie and she had no idea how to do it herself. She left the store, hoping she'd got his sizing right. She really wanted him to look as smart as possible this evening. It was Zach's big night and the least they could do was to show him proper support.

She made it back to the hotel by four o'clock.

On picking up the tickets from reception, she was panicked to see they had to be at the gate to be let in to the Palais de Festivals by six thirty, at the latest. They'd be wise to grab a bite to eat before that because she wasn't sure whether there'd be food at the party and if there was, they probably wouldn't get their hands on any of it until late in the evening.

The party started at nine o'clock, so it looked as though they were expected to go straight from the premiere to the yacht where it was being held, ready to set sail for the evening on the stroke of nine.

Despite her worry about Adam and what she'd seen earlier, she felt a surge of excitement at the thought of the evening ahead. She'd never been invited to anything so glamorous before. Even working in the radio industry, nothing as sensational as this had happened to her.

So, this was it. Her one and only chance to feel like a movie star.

* * *

After taking another shower, she dried and styled her hair so it fell in soft waves around her face and bounced around her shoulders. The front she clipped up in a few places to give the style a bit of height and she swept her heavy fringe to one side, giving it some texture with some hair wax she found in Adam's washbag.

She was pleased with the result and finished the look with dark kohl around her eyes and a heavy coat of mascara that made her eyelashes look full and incredibly long.

Checking her phone, she felt a surge of unease about how late it was getting. Adam still wasn't back and he was cutting it close now to get ready in time.

Pushing her worry away – telling herself that was his problem – she dropped the dress carefully over her head, then applied a final coat of deep red lipstick. Finally, she put on the beautiful friendship knot necklace that Zach had given her. Going to look in the long mirror in the bedroom, she studied the results. She looked good, if she did say so herself. Like a sophisticated and stylish woman. She smiled at her reflection and saw her eyes sparkle back at her.

She couldn't believe how lucky she was to be here. It was like a dream.

The door to the living area slamming shut broke her out of her contemplation and she swished into the room to find that Adam had finally arrived back.

He was drunk again.

He swayed in front of her, his hair windswept and his clothes rumpled.

Daisy took a deep breath, determined not to get angry and allow him to ruin her night before it even began.

'Where the hell did you get to?' he asked her crossly. He was really drunk. Stumbling drunk. He staggered in and landed heavily on the sofa. Daisy knew she'd have to take full blame for not turning up at the Petite Majestic earlier if they weren't going to get into a fight about this now and potentially miss both the premiere and possibly the party too.

They'd be able to work it out afterwards – hopefully when he'd sobered up.

'I'm so sorry,' she said, holding both hands up in

apology. 'I lost track of time, then got really lost on my way back and by the time I got to the bar, you must have gone,' she lied, hoping desperately that he hadn't been at the Petite Majestic all afternoon and had just come from there. 'I would have called but I forgot to take my mobile with me.' At least this part was true. In her haste to leave that morning, she'd forgotten to pick it up from the nightstand.

'Humph,' he muttered. From his lack of reaction, he obviously had been somewhere else.

Where would that have been? Daisy wondered, before pushing the thought to the back of her mind. It didn't matter right now; what mattered was persuading Adam to get ready, sobering him up and jollying him out of his bad mood so that they could enjoy the evening.

'What have you been doing all afternoon?' she asked, tentatively.

'Just hanging out with some guys I met in the bar. When you didn't show, they took me to some place on the edge of town,' he muttered noncommittally. Daisy decided to ignore the blatant lie for now. 'I can't believe I got stood up by my own girlfriend,' he continued, clearly not willing to let her transgression go without making her feel really shitty about it.

She decided she wasn't going to let him do that

to her though, especially when she'd seen him with that woman, so she ignored this. 'I've ordered some sandwiches from room service. We need to eat quickly and get going. The doors open at six thirty and we can't be late,' she said, hoping against hope he'd be reasonable about it.

'I'm not hungry,' he replied, sinking further back onto the sofa.

Daisy tamped down her annoyance. She was determined to get him dressed and out of the door without causing a row.

'Okay,' she said reasonably. 'Just jump in the shower and get dressed then.'

'In a minute,' he said waving her away like she was some pesky nag.

Her blood started to boil.

Keep calm, Daisy.

She glanced at the clock, her stomach lurching when she saw it was now eight minutes past six.

They weren't going to make it at this rate.

'Adam, we have to be there in twenty minutes so you need to get dressed now!' It was impossible to stop the anger pervading her voice now.

He looked at her with a scornful expression. 'Okay, keep your hair on,' he said, rousing himself and sloping off into the bathroom.

As he passed her, Daisy caught a whiff of perfume in the air around him. It was sweet, like honey, with an undertone of roses. She could guess where he'd picked that up.

She paced whilst waiting for him, munching on the odd sandwich, her appetite now very small, and watching the clock tick down until the time the film started.

Finally, he came out of the bathroom and pulled on the dinner jacket and trousers that she'd hired for him, grumbling the whole time about how his suit would have been perfectly fine. Luckily, it all fit. The collar on the shirt was a bit tight, but at that point, Daisy didn't care one bit. *He should have come with me to get it*, she thought angrily to herself, *instead of chatting someone up in a bar.*

'You look good,' she told him once he was dressed. And he did. He looked dashing in his get-up and for a second, Daisy remembered why she had fallen for him in the first place.

He did up his cufflinks, not reacting to her compliment.

'Right, we're good to go,' she said, hurt at him blanking her, but relieved that they were finally ready.

She called down to reception and asked them to

arrange for a car to take them to the Palais de Festival, even though it was only a short walk. She didn't think she'd be able to manage it in her heels. Plus, they were running really late now and wouldn't make it otherwise.

She checked she had the tickets, then put her shoes on, wobbling slightly at the height. After one final check in the mirror, she grabbed her bag and ushered Adam out of the room.

He was still clearly drunk and finding it a hard to walk straight.

Daisy cursed him silently. Why was he doing this to her? He'd never acted like this before. It was as if a doppelgänger had taken his place.

With no time to dwell on it, she pressed the button to call the lift. It occurred to her as they swooped downwards that Adam hadn't made any mention about how she looked. This realisation stung. In the past he'd been really attentive and sweet when she made an effort to get dressed up.

Still smarting, she led him through the foyer and out into the balmy night air. The concierge had found a car for them and they jumped in it. The driver made slow progress down the Croisette, due to the large numbers of people making their way towards the red-carpet show before the premiere, so they were able to clearly see the Cinema de la plage, a large screen set up on the beach, where crowds were already assembling to watch a movie that evening under the stars, with the gentle lull of the sea rolling faintly in the background.

* * *

The car finally drew up to the side entrance of the red-carpet walkway and Daisy and Adam got out.

After showing their tickets to the lady on the gate, they were ushered through quickly.

They were cutting it pretty fine.

The cars that were transporting the stars of the film to the premiere were already arriving, and Daisy was aware of a rise in noise level as the first actors began to make their way along the start of the red carpet.

It was a very long walk from the end, up to the steps and into the Palais and Daisy was glad she and Adam were joining it half way up. She didn't know how she was going to manage the stairs in her shoes and she knew she couldn't rely on Adam to help her as he was having enough trouble keeping himself straight. She was going to have to take it slowly.

As they mounted the steps, there was a low

murmur from the press core to their left. Daisy looked over to see them talking amongst themselves, trying to decide whether she and Adam were famous or not. One of them obviously decided that they might be and started to take photos of them calling, 'Give us a smile, beautiful. Over here!'

As soon as his flash went off, all the other photographers assumed she must be worth taking a photo of too and nearly blinded them with a riot of flashes.

Turning away to blink the light out of her eyes, Daisy was shocked to see their progress up the red-carpet steps was being broadcast on an enormous screen to the masses of fans waiting below to catch a glimpse of the film's stars. Her stomach rolled at the thought. How did Zach cope with this kind of thing all the time? She guessed he must just be used to it by now.

They finally made it to the top of the steps and Daisy turned at the last minute to see a group of actors – was Zach with them? She couldn't quite see from where she stood – making their way up the red carpet, much to the delight of the crowds and the waiting media. Before she was able to locate him, she and Adam were quickly ushered in through the door and directed towards their seats. They were up

in the gods and Daisy felt slightly dizzy as she shuffled past rows of people's legs in her heels to find
where they were sitting.

Once there, she stood for a second, looking down
over the balcony that separated them from the floor,
to see if she could make out where Zach would be
sitting, but it was impossible to tell from that
distance.

As she sat down, she noticed with a cringe of embarrassment that the cinema screen in front of them
was also playing the live feed from the cameras outside and realised that their stumbling progress up
the steps had also just been watched by a cinema full
of people.

Her humiliation was short-lived though because
as she continued to gaze at the screen, she finally
caught sight of Zach making his way past the fans
and the photographers. He looked incredible. His
beautifully cut dinner jacket emphasising the width
of his shoulders and the stark white shirt against his
bronzed skin made him look healthy and vital. His
dark eyes held a warm smile for the crowds and he
raised a hand to wave at his adoring fans.

Daisy watched him in awe, floored that this was
Zach, her childhood friend and first ever lover. Her
whole body appeared to be trembling now and a

deep throb, low in her pelvis, was sending waves of pure, anticipatory pleasure cascading through her body.

He was literally taking her breath away.

She felt Adam shift uncomfortably in the seat next to her. There wasn't a lot of leg room and his long legs were cramped in the space it allowed. He slumped down as far as he could and lay his head on her shoulder. She shrugged him off in annoyance.

'Adam, sit up will you and give me some space. You're making me really uncomfortable,' she hissed. She desperately needed her personal space right now. Her body was experiencing all sorts of crazy sensations and she needed every ounce of willpower to stop herself from leaping out of her seat and rushing off to find somewhere quiet to calm her racing thoughts.

Adam shifted back into an upright position, grumbling at her rejection.

'When's this bloody film going to start?' he muttered.

She just ignored him and continued to watch the screen. A beautiful woman had joined Zach on the red carpet and had taken his hand in a proprietary gesture, now walking at his side, waving to the crowds. She and Zach looked the picture of a happy couple and for a horrible second, Daisy wondered whether they were in a relationship. But how could they be? Surely, he would have mentioned it to her?

'Is that his new bird?' Adam muttered, staring at the screen now too. 'Nice.'

Daisy glanced at him in annoyance but didn't reply, blood pounding in her head.

The rest of the stars of the film, as well as the producers and director, were now traversing the red carpet after them and the cameras followed their progress until they walked through the doors into the Palais.

There was a hubbub of chatter from the floor below them and Daisy guessed from the raised voices and clapping that the stars and crew had entered the cinema and were taking their seats.

She strained to see if she could make out where Zach was sitting, but it was impossible to see him from where she was. She slumped back into her seat in disappointment.

A hush suddenly fell amongst the audience and a man with ruffled, titian-coloured hair, dressed in a navy-blue suit and crisp white shirt – which was open at the neck and without a tie, in clear contravention of tradition here – walked up onto the stage in front of the screen and gave a nod of greeting as the whole audience clapped loudly.

'Thank you, and thanks for joining us here tonight. For those of you that don't know me, I'm Jon, the director of this movie. I hate making speeches so I'll spare you. I just want to say thanks to everyone involved; I couldn't have done it without you. Without further ado, I give you *Damascus Days*.'

As he walked off the stage, the lights dimmed and the projectionist started the print rolling.

Daisy's nerves were jangling in anticipation of what she was about to watch. How would it make her feel to see Zach up there on the big screen in all his charismatic glory? She'd deliberately not watched any of the films or shows he'd been in up to this point, finding the idea of it too weird and discombobulating. But here it felt different. She wanted to support her friend in his professional capacity and be able to tell him what a great job he'd done without having to lie about having seen his work.

And at least here she could stare at his captivating face for a couple of hours without raising any suspicions about how her body responded to him.

At this anguished thought, she glanced over at Adam and was annoyed to see that he'd fallen asleep. He let out a loud snore and she poked him hard in the ribs.

'Adam, for God's sake, wake up!' she hissed. He jolted awake with a start and looked at her blearily. She shook her head at him, then turned back to the film as the title credits came up on the screen.

Pleasure twisted through her as Zach's name appeared and she experienced a rush of pride that she knew him.

The film began then and she settled in to it, soon losing herself in the plot, only occasionally brought up short by the notion that it was *Zach* on the screen.

The beautiful woman from the red carpet played his love interest and Daisy found herself digging her nails into her palms when it came to the sex scene, having to consciously unclasp her hands and remind herself that it wasn't real.

She, on the other hand, had experienced the real thing.

Her stomach gave a flip at the memory of his mouth on hers and the way he'd moved inside her with such need and possessive pleasure, before she forced the images from her mind. That hadn't exactly been real either. Over the years, the memory had taken on a surreal shape, so she wasn't entirely sure how much of it had really happened and how much was fanciful reminiscence.

Part way through the film, Adam had fallen asleep again but this time, she left him to his slumber. At least this way, he might be sober enough for the party afterwards.

When the end credits finally rolled on the screen, Daisy found she was devastated it was finished. It'd been a really engaging film. Both Zach and his co-star had been excellent in their parts and fingering the friendship knot on her necklace, she felt another rush of pride for being lucky enough to be part of his life.

When the lights came back up, she nudged Adam awake and he opened his bloodshot eyes and peered at her.

'Is it over?' he asked groggily.

'Yes,' she snapped. He really was the worst.

'Come on,' she said, motioning for him to stand up. 'We need to get over to where the yacht's docked before it sets sail.'

Adam yawned and rubbed his hand over his eyes then over his scalp, making his hair stand on end.

'Come on then, let's go,' he sighed, clearly not enamoured about the idea of a *party on a yacht*. What the hell was wrong with him?

Getting up and stretching his arms above his head, he shuffled down the aisle in front of her and they joined the queue of people making slow progress out of the cinema, due to it having been a full house. There was high-spirited hubbub of chatter about the film all around her, which Daisy took to mean everyone else had enjoyed it too.

She was so pleased for Zach. Perhaps an Oscar nomination would be on the way? She hoped so. He deserved it.

Adam looked around him, seemingly still in a bit of a daze, as they exited into the balmy night air.

'I think it's this way,' Daisy said, motioning towards the dock that ran along the back of the Palais de Festival. They walked as quickly as Daisy's shoes would allow over to where a huge yacht was tethered. As they approached the roped-off footbridge to the yacht, they were hindered by a large group of people that had gathered, trying desperately to get into the party without tickets. A scary-looking bouncer was keeping them at bay with a hard stare, but he moved to one side to let Daisy and Adam pass when they held out their invitations to him.

They walked carefully up the gangplank and onto the plush yacht which was already filling up with guests.

'Right, I'm off to find the bar,' Adam said abruptly, leaving her standing there on her own, feeling a bit flustered and nervous, not to mention cross with him for abandoning her.

'It's the only way to ward off this oncoming hang-over,' he called back to her over his shoulder.

She watched him go, weaving amongst the crowd of well-dressed guests, drawing both inquisitive and scornful looks from the partygoers at the way he was staggering around.

Daisy flushed with embarrassment for him – and for herself to be seen to be here with him in that state – and looked around to find a quiet corner where she could blend into the furniture until Adam arrived back with drinks. At least she hoped he was getting a drink for her.

She watched in awe as the other guests chatted away confidently, feeling a little inadequate compared to the sophisticated gathering. Many of them were obviously very powerful in their field and they gave off strong vibes of self-possession and command.

Daisy had never seen so many beautiful people in one place before either; each one was as polished and stylish as the next and even in her couture gown, she began to feel a little clumsy and uncouth in comparison. So, she was relieved to see Adam making his way back through the crowd, a bottle of wine and two glasses clutched in his hands.

'Here you go. It's complimentary so I took the whole bottle,' he said with glee.

Daisy cringed at his crassness, but accepted the proffered glass. The alcohol warmed her insides as it slipped down and she began to feel renewed flutters of excitement as she relaxed a little and looked out for Zach arriving.

She didn't have to wait long.

There was a murmur amongst the crowd and he suddenly appeared, shaking hands and accepting compliments about his performance.

As she watched, he looked around, searching for something, or someone, until his gaze alighted on her. His eyes widened for a moment at the sight of her before he smiled his incredible smile and she felt her insides melt under his gaze.

He turned back for a moment to answer a question that was being asked of him by a tall, elegant, blonde woman, then excused himself and made his way over towards where Daisy and Adam sat, a look of pure relief on his face at seeing them.

'Adam, Daisy, great, you're here,' he said with a sigh, flopping down onto the sofa next to Adam. 'I thought I was going to have to spend the whole evening swapping small talk. I guess that's the problem with mixing business with pleasure,' he said under his breath, grinning at them. 'What?' he asked, bemused by their dumbfounded response.

Adam recovered himself first. 'Yeah, what a shit life you lead, mate,' he muttered, shifting away from Zach on the sofa.

Daisy frowned at him, embarrassed by his drunken sarcasm. 'It's just so strange to see you like this, amongst these people, that is,' she said, desperately trying to salvage the situation and get them all back on a friendly keel. 'I can't get used to you being famous,' she finished lamely.

'Yeah, well, it's not all it's cut out to be,' he said, frowning at Adam. 'What did you think of the film? Be honest, I can take it.' His expression was expectant, though; he was obviously hoping for a positive response.

Adam just shrugged. 'I don't know. I slept through most of it,' he said. 'Sorry, mate.' The apology was made without much conviction.

Daisy stiffened in anger at this cruel response. How could he be so rude and uncaring towards his best friend? But she knew why he was being like this. He was jealous of Zach's success.

Zach's face was a mask of nonchalance, but Daisy saw the hurt flash in his eyes.

'Yeah, well, I guess it's not everyone's cup of tea,' he muttered.

'Well, I loved it, and I thought you were brilliant in it,' Daisy said, giving him a heartfelt smile and hoping she could undo some of the damage Adam had wreaked. She knew how she'd feel if it was her receiving such a damning review of her work at the radio station and she desperately wanted to save Zach the pain.

'Thank you, Daisy,' he said with real warmth in his voice. 'And you look beautiful in that dress. I knew you would.' He smiled now, the expression in his eyes genuine.

She smiled back, warmed by his praise.

Zach's attention was suddenly drawn away by his co-star arriving beside him.

Daisy gazed up at her from her lowly position on the sofa.

The woman was radiant. Her flawless skin glowed with health and she projected an enviable, comfortable-in-her-own skin vibe.

'Hey,' Zach said, 'let me introduce you to Savannah.' He turned back to his co-star. 'This is Daisy and this is Adam,' Zach said, gesturing towards them in turn. 'They're two of my oldest friends,' he added, slapping Adam gently on the arm.

Adam just glared at him and leaned away.

Daisy tried desperately to keep her face neutral and friendly whilst shaking hands with the stunning, somewhat other-worldly-looking actor.

'Hi there, great to meet you. Zach's told me a lot about you both,' Savannah said, apparently unaware of the uncomfortable atmosphere that had fallen between them all.

'Zach, have you seen Jon? He said he'd meet me here, but I can't find him anywhere,' she said scanning the crowd that had gathered behind her, all desperate for a moment of her time.

'No, sorry,' Zach said, shaking his head. 'He could be in the bar area. I'm sure he made it on board though, don't worry.' He gave her a reassuring smile.

'Yeah, I'm sure he did,' she agreed, somewhat placated. 'I'm just going to check over there,' she said. 'Excuse me. It was great meeting you both,' she directed this towards Adam and Daisy, before gliding off to the bar, a sea of admirers following in her wake.

'She's madly in love with the director and they're

having a bit of a shit time of it at the moment,' Zach confided under his breath.

Daisy experienced a rush of relief at this information. So, Savannah and Zach *weren't* together.

Someone executive-looking came over then. 'Zach, great performance. I have a new project coming up that might interest you...'

Daisy took the opportunity, while Zach's attention was otherwise engaged, to chastise Adam for his behaviour.

'What the hell's the matter with you!' she hissed, glaring at him.

Adam just shrugged at her. 'Just look at him, Daisy. He thinks he's some kind of god parading around here. Wanker. And you're just making a fool of yourself sucking up to him like a groupie,' he added, clearly well on his way to being drunk again.

But before Daisy could respond to this nonsense, Zach turned back to them.

'Sorry about that, I guess I'm still working,' he said with a roll of his eyes.

'You really are a good actor, you know,' she blurted, a little wildly.

'For fuck's sake, Daisy,' Adam muttered, glaring at her.

She felt like kicking him.

'What's your fucking problem, Adam?' Zach asked suddenly, his eyes flashing with irritation at his friend's vindictive behaviour.

Adam just glared back at him with a sardonic grin on his face. 'You know exactly what my problem is,' he snapped back.

'What's going on here?' Daisy asked, suddenly struck by the fact she was missing a step. What were they talking about?

Zach glanced at her, then held up his hands in a placating gesture towards Adam. 'Look, why don't we go and get you another drink at the bar?' he suggested, nodding at Adam's now empty glass, clearly trying to defuse the situation.

'I don't need you getting me *shit*. I'll go on my own,' Adam stated, standing up and striding away, careering into people as he went.

'Adam, wait,' Zach said, throwing Daisy a look that said *stay here, I've got this*, before getting up too and following him through the crowd towards the bar.

Daisy watched them go. Perhaps Zach would be able to get through to him; she certainly didn't seem to be having any luck.

Just then, she felt a tap on her shoulder and swivelled round to see the man from the café standing there, grinning at her. He looked fantastic in his tuxedo, very dashing, and Daisy was momentarily awed at the sight of him. He really was very handsome, but in a much more traditional way than Zach and Adam. Like an old school movie star.

'Daisy, how lovely to see you again,' he drawled in his mid-Atlantic accent, moving round to sit on the sofa next to her, without bothering to ask if she minded if he sat down this time.

The sheer bloody confidence of the guy was astounding.

'Sonny. Hi,' she said, raising a hand in greeting and once again feeling slightly uncomfortable under his intense gaze.

'So, did you enjoy the film?' he asked.

'Yes, I thought it was fantastic,' she admitted, nodding. She probably should at least be civil before she escaped, just in case he was a friend of Zach's.

'Not one of the director's best,' he said, giving what seemed to her to be a disingenuous smile. 'But a good effort all round, I thought.'

Daisy wasn't sure about his tone. Something about it didn't ring true.

She was distracted by a tall figure looming over them and Daisy turned to see Zach standing at the end of the sofa, watching them with a dark frown on his face. Perhaps he'd not been able to get through to Adam after all.

'Ah, the man of the moment,' Sonny said, holding out his hand to Zach for it to be shaken.

Zach grasped it for a moment, shaking it abruptly before pulling his hand away and nodding curtly at the other man.

Sonny clearly sensed Zach wasn't in the mood for chitchat because he excused himself and after leaning over to kiss Daisy on the cheek – which she was too surprised by to react to immediately – backed away from them with a grin, striding off towards the other side of the boat.

Zach watched him go, his frown still very much in place.

'Where's Adam?' Daisy asked.

'I left him at the bar. I don't know what's got into him,' he confided with a grimace. 'He seems really angry with me about something, but he won't tell me what.'

'Yeah, I'm sorry about that. We had a bit of a row about coming out this evening after I stood him up for lunch. I think he's feeling miffed about not being able to do exactly what *he* wants every second of the day. But then, I guess it's his holiday too, so maybe he has a point,' she said, putting a hand on his arm for reassurance.

Zach looked at her steadily for a moment before saying, 'Sod it, let's leave him to have some fun on his own then. Come and dance with me.'

Before she could react, he grabbed her hand and pulled her up off the sofa, towing her towards a dance floor on the other side of the boat. It was already full of couples gliding around the floor to a slow jazz number being played by a cool-looking band set up on a raised stage. Nervous excitement rushed through her as Zach wrapped his arms around her back and guided her into the middle of the throng, where they swayed together, their bodies pressed close.

She caught sight of the bright lights of the Cannes shoreline flash by in the distance as he slowly turned her, leading the movement and melding her into his body.

Her breath shortened and her head began to swim with the intensity of her response to him holding her so close, his scent wrapping around her senses and his breath ruffling her hair. The unnerving throb began to pulse, deep inside her again, sending tendrils of need through every part of her body, and she pressed herself closer to him, drinking him in and revelling in the wild joy he was provoking.

'I knew you'd be a great dancer,' he murmured into her ear. 'That's one of the things I love about you: the way you move. You carry yourself with such grace.'

Daisy drew back to look into his eyes, the expression she found there intense but unfathomable. She felt swallowed up by the depth of this enigmatic feeling. She was out of control, miles away in her head, lost in sensation.

Then suddenly, rudely, she was jerked out of her hypnotised state by Adam pulling roughly on her arm, tearing her from Zach's grip and almost sending her spinning across the floor in her heels.

Looking into his face, she saw intense fury there and her stomach rolled with anxiety.

'Get your fucking hands off her, Dryden!' he raged at his friend. Bringing his arm back, he swung his fist hard into Zach's jaw.

There was a sickening crack and Zach stumbled backwards, taken completely off guard by the attack. After regaining his balance, he turned to stare at Adam, a look of disbelief and controlled anger in his eyes.

'What the fuck was that for?'

'You just couldn't leave her alone, could you?' Adam shouted, his voice shaking with anger. 'What? Not going to deny it?' His tone was coldly patronising now.

Zach held up his hands in defence. 'I don't know what you think's going on, but I can assure you that nothing is,' he said, his voice level.

Daisy could sense he was fighting hard to control his temper as well as his distress at fighting like this with his best friend.

Adam swung round to look at Daisy now, seeming to be demanding an explanation from her as well.

'None of this is Daisy's fault. It's mine,' Zach said, directing Adam's attention back to him. 'I just wanted to make things okay with us all again. We're just friends, Adam, I swear. I wouldn't do that to you.'

'Yeah, sure, you fucking liar!' Adam spat, moving towards him menacingly. Zach backed away slowly, his hands still up in defence.

'How could you think I wouldn't notice?' Adam said, his voice breaking with emotion.

Zach shook his head, then took a steadying breath and looked directly at his friend, as if he'd changed his mind about something. 'You're not good for her, Ad. You suck all the fire out of her,' he said quietly, his voice shaking now.

'What the hell are you talking about? We're great together,' Adam spat back at him. 'You really think she'd be better off with you! You've no idea how to love another person.'

Zach looked like he'd been smacked in the face again and stared back at his friend with a wretched expression.

There was a moment of silence between them. Nobody moved or said anything, the anticipation in the air thick.

Seeming to decide there was nothing he could say to make things better right now, Zach turned away and pushed through the crowd, leaving Adam standing there in a passionate fury.

'Go on then, you fucking coward. Run away, just like you always do!' Adam yelled at his retreating back. Then spinning around, he turned back to face Daisy, looking at her with such a cold expression, she felt a shiver run down her spine.

'As for you, you treacherous bitch...' he began, but he suddenly seemed to run out of words. He stared at her for a long moment, his eyes so full of pain, it took Daisy's breath away.

She put her hand out to reach for him, to try to

soothe him in some way, but he just looked at it as if it was something filthy and turning on his heel, strode away from her, forcing his way through the crowd that had gathered to watch in awed silence.

Daisy was aware of a rising murmur of voices and heard a couple of people behind her murmur, 'How embarrassing.'

'What happened?'

'It's her fault, apparently. They were fighting over her.'

'*Her*? Really?'

Humiliation crashed over her as she was suddenly confronted by the realisation that she was now completely alone, standing there in the middle of a crowd of unfriendly strangers who were staring at her in fascinated mirth.

Fear quickly followed. What was she going to do? She was trapped on a boat full of people who didn't know or care about her, with no way of getting away from the awful scene that had just played out.

Panic started to rise in her chest and she looked around desperately for a way out of there. A strong, warm hand suddenly closed over her arm and she was relieved to see a familiar face smiling down at her. She allowed herself to be led away from the crowd and into the corner of the bar area, behind a partition, where she was gently guided down into a seat and a glass of, what looked like, champagne put into her hand.

She took a large gulp of it, but her hand was shaking so much, she nearly spilled what was left of it onto her dress, and was grateful when it was taken away from her and put onto a nearby table, before the liquid could ruin the beautiful material.

She turned to face out towards the sea for a moment to steady herself and noticed with a rush of relief that the yacht was pulling into the harbour.

'Daisy? Are you okay?' Sonny asked, looking at her with what looked like genuine concern in his stunning golden eyes. He'd rescued her, she realised now. She'd probably still be standing there like a lemon, in the grip of a panic attack, if it hadn't been for him. Taking a deep breath, she fought back the tears that were threatening to spill down her cheeks and nodded, giving him a shaky smile.

'I'm okay,' she whispered, not feeling it in the least. 'Have you seen Zach anywhere?'

He looked back at her steadily, his Hollywood-handsome face a picture of concern.

'No, sorry.' He smoothed the back of his hand over her cheek. 'You poor darling. Come here,' he said, gently pulling her towards him and enveloping her in a tight hug.

She stiffened at first, but after a moment relaxed into the comfort of the embrace. But she only had a moment of feeling safe in his arms before he pulled away from her and gazed into her eyes again.

'Hey, it's going to be okay. None of this is your fault,' he reassured her.

'It's all my fault,' she said with a small hiccough of shame.

He wrinkled his nose. 'Nah. Well, apart from being too beautiful and driving us guys crazy with your super-cute charm.'

Even though she baulked at this cheesy line, she still felt the warmth of his compliment soak through her. It was like a lifeline at that moment, giving her a glimpse of safety after the terror of potentially losing the two people who meant most to her in the world.

The look Sonny was giving her was fascinating. She felt hypnotised by his shameless stare, his pupils dilated as he gazed into her eyes.

She was only aware of his mouth, hard on hers, a moment after their lips connected.

In a stunned daze, not helped by the alcohol, and the adrenaline and fear she'd been feeling only moments ago, she went with it, letting him kiss her. The feeling of being wanted and cared for but at the same time disgusted with herself for giving in to her base need made her thoughts swim to Zach, and for one intangible moment, she imagined it was him she was kissing.

'What the *fuck's* going on here?' A deep, harsh, very familiar sounding voice broke into her trance-like state.

She jerked away from the kiss, shocked and a bit discombobulated to find herself in Sonny's arms.

Zach stood over them, his body language emanating vibes of rage.

Nausea swelled in Daisy's stomach as she took in the look of utter disgust on his face.

She shrank away from the ferocity of his gaze, intensely aware of how hard-pressed-up to Sonny she was on the sofa.

'Uh, I think I'll leave you two to it,' Sonny said quietly, but with a disconcerting smirk on his face. He drew away from her and got up in one fluid motion, then strode off, not looking back.

Daisy watched him go, eking out the time before she had to turn and confront Zach's wrath.

'I just lost my best friend, defending you!' He hissed angrily when she finally forced herself to look at him. His eyes flashed with intense disgust. 'And you go and throw yourself at a wanker like him right afterwards. I didn't think you had stars in your eyes, Daisy, but I was obviously wrong,' he spat at her.

'What are you talk—?'

But he cut her off. 'You're doing this to get back at me, aren't you? Did you have this planned from the start? All that doe-eyed innocence; you should give acting a go, you'd be great.'

'Don't be ridi—'

He just talked over her. 'I'm not falling for it any more, Daisy. I'm done with this – with *you*.'

Then before she could even respond, he turned and walked away.

Daisy felt as though he'd just slapped her in the face. She sat there in stupefied shock for a moment, unable to believe that had all just happened, until she gathered her wits about her, got up on wobbly legs and ran after him as fast as she could in her ridiculously high heels.

Zach was striding onto the walkway that linked the yacht with the mainland when she caught up with him.

'What the hell are you talking about?' she said, grabbing his arm to stop him, urging him to turn and face her. 'I don't even know him. I only met him today.'

He stared at her in disbelief for a moment, then looked down with distaste at her hand still on his arm and shrugged her off.

'Don't touch me,' he said with such ferocity, she took a step backwards.

She'd never seen him so angry and was shocked by the intensity of it. His whole body appeared taut with rage.

'He came on to me!' she shouted, fury at the injustice of it all making her voice shrill.

'Yeah, sure. You didn't look like you were struggling too hard to me.' He took a deliberate step away from her. 'You're just a manipulative, self-serving bitch and always have been. Just fuck off and leave me alone, Daisy.' This was said directly into her face, the expression in his eyes hard and cold.

It cut straight through her, making her entire body cold with icy dread.

She couldn't believe he could speak to her like that, after all they'd shared over the last couple of days.

'So much for friendship.' Her voice was shaking with emotion now and she glared at him defiantly, determined not to let him intimidate her. 'Here,' she said pulling the friendship knot away from her throat and snapping the delicate chain, holding it out to him. 'You'd better have this back.'

Zach just looked at it steadily, his eyes hard.

'You keep it. It means nothing to me,' he said, without a hint of emotion in his voice.

'Fine!' she shouted and bringing her arm back, she threw it as far as she could out to sea.

They both watched as the diamond glinted briefly in the moonlight, before the necklace disappeared with a small splash into the water.

Daisy spun back to see a mixture of disbelief and fury cross Zach's face, before he turned and walked away from her, his hands bunched into fists at his sides.

Daisy slumped down onto the wooden walkway and let the tears finally flow, sobbing uncontrollably with her head in her hands.

She was aware of other people leaving the boat and stepping delicately around her, but no-one stopped to ask if she was alright.

She really was completely alone.

Eventually, once her sobs had subsided and everyone seemed to have left the boat, she picked herself up and trailed miserably back to the hotel, carrying her shoes in her hand and giving her now painful feet a break.

She got back to find the suite in darkness. Adam had obviously not come back yet.

She trailed around the place in a state of panic, her heart racing, terrified he might have done something stupid or hurt himself. Picking up her mobile, she called him with shaking fingers, but he didn't pick up and it went to answerphone.

'Adam,' she said in a quavering voice, 'where are you? I'm worried about you. Please don't have fallen overboard. Call me when you get this, okay?'

Throwing her phone onto the nightstand, she slumped onto the bed and stared up at the ceiling, willing him to respond.

Eventually, when it seemed like he wasn't calling her back any time soon, she got undressed and wiped away the make-up that now streaked her face.

Half an hour later, he still hadn't appeared or called, so she got into bed and pulled the covers up to her ears, her mind in a whirl.

Half of her didn't care what had happened to him – he'd humiliated her so completely – but the other half badly wanted him to come back.

She needed to know he was okay and even if they ended up rowing for a while, she was sure she could talk him round. He usually relented when they argued, allowing her to be the dominant one, and she desperately needed this release to help her come to terms with what had just happened.

Her desperation sickened her.

Unable to settle, she got up and paced back and forth for a while, alternately looking out of the window for any sign of him and trying his mobile, which always went straight to answerphone. After an hour of this, she gave up and fell, exhausted, into bed, telling herself it was unlikely anything really bad had happened to him. There had been so many people on board the boat and security had been all over it. Someone would have noticed if something untoward had happened.

It was much more likely he'd gone off to some late-night bar to drown his sorrows. Anyway, there was absolutely nothing she could do about it now. She had no-one else here to turn to, now that Zach had disowned her, so she'd just have to pull herself together and deal with it. Preferably in the morning after some reviving sleep.

* * *

Daisy awoke after a fitful night to find Adam still hadn't returned.

A pang of terror struck her as she tumbled out of bed, still woozy with sleep.

She checked the living area, but there was no sign that he'd come back at all.

She felt sick.

Her head throbbed and her body ached from the exertion of crying so much the night before. Looking in the mirror, she was shocked to see how swollen and bloodshot her eyes were.

Taking a shower, she tried not to move too quickly as it only made her head pound even harder.

Feeling a little better after washing away the sweat of the night before, she got dressed and tried applying some eye make-up to hide the puffiness around her eyes, but it just made her look worse, so she took it off again.

The noise of the door clicking open made her jump and she ran into the living area to see Adam stumble in, slamming the door behind him. He looked awful. His hair and clothes were a mess and his face was pale, his eyes bloodshot. He looked round to find her standing there and just stared at her blankly.

'Where have you been? I've been so worried!' She half shouted, half pleaded. He continued to look levelly at her, seemingly totally unmoved by her agitation.

Finally, he shrugged. 'I went to a bar then ended up sleeping on the beach.'

He walked over to the sofa and leaned against the back of it, folding his arms in front of him. 'I couldn't stand to be around you. You fucking *humiliated* me,' he said, glaring at her with anger in his eyes. He'd never looked at her like that before and she felt a shock of fear. Was this going to be the end of them? Surely it couldn't be?

'What about me?' she whispered. 'Don't you think I was humiliated too? You just left me there on my own, looking like a fool in front of a boat full of strangers.'

'What did you expect?' he said, glaring at her in disgust. Daisy was shocked at the coldness of his tone. This wasn't the Adam she'd known all her life.

'I don't know what you thought was happening, but I can assure you that nothing was,' she countered.

'Yeah, sure, Daisy. It looked like you were just innocently dancing with a *really good friend*.' His sarcastic tone cut right through her.

'Don't be an idiot!' she exclaimed, furious at his accusation, but at the same time feeling a flush of shame at his words. He was right, of course; there had always been something between her and Zach, even though neither of them had acknowledged it recently.

At least Adam didn't need to worry on that score any more, she thought sadly. She doubted she'd ever see anything of Zach again after the way he'd reacted last night.

'But I *am* an idiot,' he said, then sighed, his shoulders slumping in defeat. He moved round and sat down heavily on the sofa, burying his face in his hands. 'You're in love with Zach and you always have been. Not me.'

Daisy sat down next to him and put a hand out to gently touch his arm. 'That's not true,' she said, though the words felt wrong in her mouth.

'Don't touch me,' he said gruffly, moving away from her.

His rejection stung – not *him* too – but she stayed where she was and didn't try to touch him again.

After a minute's tense silence, he got up and stalked towards the bedroom.

'I'm taking a shower, then I'm going to book us onto the next flight home.' He flung these words back over his shoulder. 'Pack your things,' he commanded, walking into the bathroom and slamming the door.

Daisy winced at the sound. Her head throbbed.

But at least he hadn't just walked out and left her there on her own. He was planning on travelling home with her.

She guessed he was probably making a good call. They should get out of there now and go home, back to normality, and lick their wounds. Perhaps back in London, things wouldn't seem so desperately messed up.

The thought of going back to their flat comforted her somewhat, but she also felt a pang of regret.

Before the events of last night, she'd been in her element. She'd never had so much fun.

But it hadn't been real. It felt now like it had all been a dream. Some bits of it turning into a nightmare, of course – especially the most recent events.

With a sigh, she levered herself up from the sofa and went into the bedroom to pack.

Touching all the beautiful new clothes lovingly as she laid them carefully in her case, she tried not to think about how she'd come to own them. She'd so enjoyed buying them, but now they would only remind her of Zach.

She couldn't keep them. She'd give them away as

soon as she got home. Someone else could enjoy them; they no longer held any appeal for her.

A tear dropped from her eye and landed on the soft material of the cashmere jumper she'd coveted so much. She wiped it away gently and closed the case.

She'd leave the evening gown with reception and ask them to send it back to the shop for her. In her gut, she knew there was no chance of seeing Zach again – he was too proud. So, she'd never have the opportunity to explain to him what had really happened with Sonny.

She'd just have to lock all thoughts of him out of her head forever and be grateful for what she did have. Whatever that turned out to be.

14

Things were really rocky on the way home.

Adam studiously ignored her for the whole journey, only giving one-word answers if she asked him a question.

She gave up in the end and tried, but failed, to sleep and block out the overwhelming sadness that pervaded her. The flight seemed interminably long and Daisy was hugely relieved when the plane finally landed in London.

As soon as they set foot through the door to their flat, Adam headed off to take a shower, leaving Daisy to lug the heavy cases into the hallway. She trailed miserably into the living room and slumped down onto the sofa. After a while, she heard him exit the bathroom, then go into the spare room, slamming the door behind him. Closing her eyes, she dropped her head into her hands, overcome with exhaustion.

They were in for a pretty rough time, she felt sure of it. Adam was usually very quick to resolve any issues between them – in fact, historically, it had always been him who had pushed for a truce – but this time, it felt very different.

It was going to be tough for them to come back from this. And honestly, did she even want to?

Things hadn't been great between them for a while now, which she'd put down to a rough patch, but was it more than that? Had their relationship run its course?

How could she possibly rescue things with Adam when she was in love with someone else?

Because she was, of course. Adam had been absolutely right about that.

Her head had been a total mess, but everything was very clear now.

She was in love with Zach.

She knew it now for sure. She'd always known it, really, she finally admitted to herself.

So, she was with the wrong man.

But how on earth was she going to deal with this situation? Even though she knew she wasn't in love with Adam, she still loved him deeply as a friend and the thought of hurting him made her feel sick.

She had to finish it with him, but she didn't feel she had the emotional strength at the moment. Perhaps if she left it a few days, it would finish itself somehow.

Goddammit!

If Zach and Adam hadn't been such good friends, things might have been more clear cut.

Not that there was anything she could do about Zach. He'd made it very clear he was done with her.

Sighing, she stood up from the sofa.

She had to reconcile herself to the fact that she would never be with him. He was gone for good and it was unlikely she'd ever have cause to bump into him now that bridges were burned between him and Adam as well.

With this terrible thought circling her head, she retired to her room and slipped beneath the cold covers, hyper aware of how alone she was.

* * *

In the end, the cold silence went on between them for nearly a week, neither of them willing to make the first move and start the long and painful process of splitting up.

Daisy buried herself in work and they only saw each other in the evenings, and these appearances were few and far between from Adam, who tended to roll back in very late without explanation of where he'd been.

At first, Daisy was relieved to not have to be around him and the frosty atmosphere he brought with him, but by the end of the week, with them sleeping in separate rooms and barely communicating, she felt she had to say something about it.

He came stomping into the living room late one evening, bringing with him a smell of cigarette smoke and the scent of sweet honey and rose that brought Daisy up short. She knew she'd smelled it before and it took her a moment to realise where it had been. He'd smelt exactly the same the night of the premiere when he'd come back from the Petite Majestic, and wherever else it was he'd been that afternoon. She knew without a shadow of a doubt that he'd been with the woman she'd seen him with in the bar. The beautiful woman who'd so captivated his attention. Perhaps she was here in London, visiting a film festival that was currently running, or maybe she actually lived here and he'd kept in contact with her since meeting her in Cannes. She decided to test her theory. She didn't appear to have anything left to lose any more, after all.

'Adam, where have you been? I was expecting you back ages ago,' she said, trying to keep her voice steady.

'Out,' he stated. 'With a friend.'

'A *girl* friend?' she asked, her voice shaking a little with nerves.

He paused and it was that that told her everything she needed to know. 'Yes, a *girl* friend,' came his curt reply. He didn't look at her and she knew right in that moment that she'd lost him.

'Are you sleeping with her?' she asked, her voice wobbling with emotion. She needed to hear him say the awful words so she could finally start to move on from the implosion of their relationship.

Another pause. Then he turned to look her straight in the eye. 'Yes, Daisy, I am.' There was no remorse in his voice. So that was it. The Adam she knew had gone for good.

Daisy's knees buckled under her and she slumped back onto the sofa, her head spinning and nausea rising in her stomach. Putting her forehead onto her knees, she breathed deeply and slowly until the darkness passed.

When she raised her head, she looked directly at him and asked, 'Who is she?'

'You don't know her. I met her in Cannes the day you embarrassed me in front of a hundred people by practically fucking Zach on the dance floor.'

His words stung. She knew she'd been out of control that night and had hurt him, but he was being unfair.

Wasn't he?

Not that it mattered now, it seemed. Now he'd taken refuge in another pair of willing arms, to numb the pain she'd caused him.

'Why are you doing this to me?' she asked, her voice breaking. She was astounded at his cruelty.

Adam laughed scornfully. 'Why do you think, Daisy?' His handsome face was a mask of anger. 'You humiliated me! And I couldn't stand being number two to Zach any more.' He shook his head and she realised with a thump of pain that there were tears in his eyes now. 'I couldn't see you with him and know you were in love with him and not me. I know you have been for a very long time.'

'How did you know?' she asked quietly, shocked at this revelation.

'Because every time I so much as mentioned his name, you started vibrating.' He paused. 'Something happened between you that day you both fell in the water on the Fowey holiday, didn't it?'

Daisy sucked in a sharp breath. He knew about that too. How?

She didn't have to wait long to find out.

'Oh, come on. It was obvious. You were fine with me one minute, then after you went home with Zach that day, you changed. I lost you a long time ago and like an idiot, I thought I could win you back.' He grimaced. 'I should have left you alone after that, but I was so in love with you, I thought I could handle it. Oh, and then that awful weekend when he came to stay with that bloody nightmare, Lola, and lorded his perfect life in my face, then had the fucking nerve to tell you he'd "wanted to kiss you all day" when he thought my back was turned.'

Daisy felt a wave of shock and guilt swamp her. He knew *everything*. He must have heard them after all.

Her face must have registered her surprise because he nodded ruefully at her.

'Yeah, I saw you,' he said, confirming her fears. 'I walked in with those drinks and there you were... with him...' He looked suddenly very tired. 'I didn't know what to do. I was desperate not to lose you and I knew what a fickle bastard he was so I thought I could just ride it out and you'd come back to me when he eventually left – like he always does.' He shook his head and swiped a hand across his eyes.

'We were really drunk and... and... he was confused about... you know, Lola and—' she tried to protest, but he cut off her rambling defence.

'He just couldn't leave you alone,' he said, his voice croaky. All the anger seemed to have drained out of him now, leaving only sadness.

'Why did you agree to go to Cannes if you knew how Zach and I felt about each other?' she asked in a whisper.

'I don't know, Daisy. I guess I was just punishing myself for not being good enough for you or some such shit. Or maybe I thought we were strong enough to stand it. That you'd decide I was the right one for you after all when you saw what a self-centred arsehole he was, prancing around like a drama queen. And I wanted him to see us. Happy. Together. What an idiot.' He held up his hands in a kind of surrender. 'I know things haven't been great between us for a while, but I didn't want to face losing what we had. We're good together in lots of ways, but... not in others.' He took a shuddery breath. 'I was so sick of being unsure about everything. I needed to make something happen.' He let out a mirthless laugh. 'And I guess it did.'

He shook his head again, this time, she guessed, at himself.

'As I'm sure you remember, I didn't exactly find it easy. The only way I could deal with seeing the two of you together was to get blind drunk and stay that way.'

'Oh, Adam,' Daisy sighed, swiping tears away from her own eyes. She felt utterly wretched. 'I'm so, so sorry. I never meant to hurt you, please believe me.'

Adam sighed and waved a hand at her, batting away her apology. 'Well, it doesn't matter now. I'm over you. I'm in love with Suzie,' he stated confidently.

'Just like that? What about us?' she asked, unsteadily, still not entirely able to believe they were having this conversation. They'd been together for so long. Been through so much.

'We're over. We've been over for a while. We've just not wanted to admit it. I'm moving out.'

Daisy felt her world crashing down around her. She'd lost Zach and now Adam too. She was officially on her own.

'Okay.' She nodded miserably. She knew he had

to go; there was nothing left for him to stay for now. Deep down, she'd known too that their relationship had run its course a while ago. 'Where will you go?'

'Suzie said I can move in with her.' He paused for a moment and seemed to gather himself, even though tears were flowing freely down his face now. 'Bye, Daisy,' he said more gently now, reminding her with a pang of sadness of the old Adam. 'I'll come round for my things next week when you're at work.'

With that, he walked out, closing the front door quietly but firmly behind him.

15

Life felt very hard for a while.

Daisy took some leave from work and went to stay with her parents for a couple of weeks. It was so lovely to be looked after, like being a child again.

Her parents were obviously very worried about the state she was in. They'd tried to talk to her about what had happened but she was too ashamed and confused to tell them anything other than the sketchiest of details.

They were obviously very fond of Adam and sad to hear that they'd split up, but they assured her that her wellbeing was their top priority.

Even with this reassurance, she wasn't able to relate the whole sorry tale without bursting into tears, so they left her alone, clearly counting on her telling them when she was good and ready.

She spent her time there picking at the delicious meals her mother put in front of her, her appetite all but gone. She felt tired all the time and often retired to her bed early, sinking into the soft mattress, relieved at getting through one more day.

She mostly managed to block all thoughts of what had happened with Zach and Adam out of her mind, but occasionally, they would creep back in again and she would be overwhelmed by an ache of pain-tinged nostalgia, and a yearning for things to return to how they'd been, so strong, it would take her breath away.

But she knew there was no chance of that ever happening.

*　*　*

Arriving back home to London, she was upset to find the flat empty of Adam's things. But after having a good, hard, power cry, she started to feel a new sense of purpose sweep through her. It was time to change things up and move on.

Taking a steadying breath, she walked around the flat, mentally planning the things she would buy for it when she had the money – which probably wouldn't be for a while since she'd only just be able to cover the rent on her own for the time being. But if she got the pay rise at work that Jez had promised her, it could all be entirely her own choice, she realised. She wouldn't have to defer to anyone else's tastes or budget concerns.

There was something quite heartening about that.

As time went on, she found it was nice not to have to worry about what sort of mood Adam would be in when he came home from work, or to feel the ever-present weight of guilt whenever she looked at him.

Having never lived alone before, she found it was actually quite fun re-arranging the furniture and doing things like painting the walls, just for herself to appreciate for a change.

And the house was so much tidier without Adam in it.

But it didn't stop her from missing him.

* * *

Daisy was in the studio at the radio station, editing an interview, when Claire barged into the room.

'You still here?' her friend asked in surprise. 'You should have gone home ages ago.'

After a few months of living on her own, the initial excitement of it had started to wear off and Daisy had been staying later and later at work in order to avoid going home to an empty house in the evenings.

'Yeah, I know, I'm just going to finish this, then I'm going.' She waved a hand at the screen.

Claire looked at her for a moment, her face set in a deep frown.

'I'm worried about you, Daisy. We all are,' she said quietly. 'You've lost all your sparkle.'

She perched on the desk next to her and looked at her steadily. 'You've got to start going out again. It's not good for you to keep yourself locked away like this. Sorry to be harsh, but you've got to stop wallowing. It's been months now and you're still punishing yourself.'

Daisy had filled her in on the whole sorry tale soon after it had happened and Claire had been kind and understanding at first, but clearly now felt more drastic action was needed to coerce her friend out of her reclusive stupor.

'Look, I've been invited to this swanky media party on Friday at the Longe Lounge in Soho. I can get you onto the guest list. Come with me. We can have a few cocktails, flirt with some hot guys, it'll be good for you.' She leaned closer and waggled her eyebrows. 'I won't take no for an answer!' she finished bossily, cutting off Daisy's reply before she could refuse her.

Daisy slumped back into her seat in defeat, no match for her friend's determination.

'Okay.' She pointed a finger at her. 'But only to make you happy.'

Claire had been a rock since her split with Adam and she wanted to repay her kindness.

'Great, you can pick me up on the way then,' she said, sweeping out of the room before Daisy could say another word.

Sighing, she saved her work on the computer and turned it off. Claire was right, of course. It would be good for her to get out again. It was time. She couldn't go on moping around for the rest of her life.

She knew she'd never find anyone she could love more fiercely than Zach, or care for more deeply than Adam, *but you never know*, she thought to herself, *I might have some interesting experiences trying.*

* * *

When Friday night rolled around, Daisy found herself staring into her wardrobe and not finding a thing she wanted to wear.

It had been such a long while since she'd gone to a party, she didn't seem to own any suitable clothes for it any more.

She spent most days in jeans and t-shirts, not needing to be dressy for work, and had had a huge purge of her wardrobe when Adam left, in the vain attempt to banish memories of him and what she'd lost from her mind.

She hadn't been shopping since – hadn't had the energy for it – and so was now in the challenging position of making herself look decent for a party at a swanky, private members bar which was bound to be full of flashy media types in cutting-edge couture.

Dropping her gaze to the floor of the messy wardrobe, it alighted on her case, which was stashed right at the back. She pulled it out, throwing it onto the bed and opening it. The clothes she'd bought in Cannes were still in it.

She hadn't got round to giving them away yet. She'd promised herself she would, but actually doing it had been too much of a wrench in her desperately sad state.

Touching the delicate, expensive material of the

outfits, she felt a surge of sudden anger. Why had all this happened to her? She was generally a good, kind, thoughtful person who, yes, sure, had made some questionable choices, but why did they have to come back and bite her so hard?

Though Claire was probably right; it was time to stop beating herself up. You had to make your own luck, right?

She pulled a short, flared skirt out of the case and examined it. It was made of a fluid sort of material which fell into a beautiful shape when worn, the back of it dipping in behind her buttocks to cup her bottom, which gave her a striking, curvy outline.

Pulling off her dressing gown, she stepped into it. It fell to just above her knees and felt amazing as it swished against her skin. She twirled around in front of the mirror and admired it on her body. It suited her so well. It had classic lines, but the stark, colourful pattern gave it a contemporary edge.

Riffling through the case, she found the soft, long-sleeved top that went really well with it. It had a sharp, V-cut neckline and flowing sleeves, that ended with a ruffle around her wrists.

Looking at herself in the mirror in it, the outfit really drew attention to how much weight she'd lost recently and she reprimanded herself for getting into this state.

This was ridiculous.

Enough was enough.

It was time to get her life back.

With that thought ringing through her head, she strode into the bathroom to do her make-up and hair, determined to look like the self-assured woman she knew was still there inside her.

No more bloody pining.

She was going to have some fun tonight.

16

The cab pulled up on a Soho side street and Claire and Daisy got out, looking around them.

They walked past a number of innocuous-looking doors until Claire stopped in front of one of them, pointing at it.

'I'm pretty sure it's this one,' she said, 'They never have signs outside these places.' She rolled her eyes. 'I did warn you it'd be swanky.' Crossing her fingers, she pressed the buzzer on the intercom located on the wall next to them.

There was a crackle, then a voice said, 'Yes, may I help you?'

'We're here for the "Ah Vienna" party. Claire

Newsome and Daisy Malone, we're on the guest list,' Claire said into the panel.

'Just a minute,' came the reply. They could hear a clack of fingernails on a keyboard in the background. 'Okay, come on in,' the voice finally said.

The door buzzed open and they walked inside and over to a small, simple, oak reception desk with just a laptop and a big, old-fashioned ledger on it.

'Let me take your coats,' said the pretty, suit-clad girl on the desk. 'And sign in here please,' she added, motioning to the ledger. They wrote their names in it – so *old skool* – handed over their coats and climbed the winding stairs up to the next level, where the party was being held. The large room, which had a bar bang slap in the middle of it, was already thronged with people and Daisy felt the rush of warmth from so many bodies envelop her.

There was a sweet, musky undertone in the air – a mixture of all the different scents that everyone was wearing – which made her feel slightly heady. She didn't recognise anyone there, she realised with a rush of relief, so she could always just have a couple of drinks with Claire and then make her excuses, if necessary.

Claire turned to her. 'I'm just going to see if Russ is here,' she said. 'Will you be okay for a minute?'

'Of course,' Daisy said. 'Go. I'll be here, probably still queuing to get myself a drink from that very busy-looking bar.'

She smiled and winked confidently at her friend to assure her she wasn't about to leg it if left on her own for two minutes.

She got in line for the bar and was standing awkwardly behind a big group of people who all seemed to know each other, feeling a bit lost and nervous, when Zach walked into the room.

It seemed like everyone around her turned to look at him, Daisy included.

Her heart gave a hard throb in her chest and she suddenly felt as if all the air had been sucked out of the room and she couldn't breathe.

She needed to sit down.

Unfortunately, the empty chair that had been to the right of her at a deserted table a moment ago had just been moved, so when she went to half-blindly sit on it, there was nothing there to meet her bottom. She stumbled, shocked by the lack of solid object that her brain told her was still there, then, unable to right herself in her heels, fell over onto the floor with a thump.

So, the first Zach saw of her was of her flat on her

back, her floaty skirt up around her waist, flashing her knickers at him.

Her face flushed with embarrassment and she scrambled to sit up and pull her skirt down to her knees before starting to get up with as much dignity as she could manage, which wasn't much, under the circumstances.

What were the bloody odds that he'd be here, at a random private party that she'd only agreed to go to at the last minute?

And how on *earth* was she going to handle this situation?

After her last encounter with him, she'd fully expected never to see him again.

It seemed as though he was thinking the same thing because his face had registered shock when he caught sight of her, but, in his Zach-like manner, he'd quickly composed himself and strolled over.

'Dizzy, fancy seeing you here,' he said coolly, but with a glint of amusement in his eye.

It seemed like a long time since she'd heard her pet name. For some reason, she suddenly found she loved hearing it again, especially from him. It was their private joke. A thing that still bonded them.

A feeling akin to nostalgia washed over her, making her skin prickle.

He held out a hand and not knowing what else to do, she allowed him to pull her back up to standing.

Straightening her skirt, she took a moment to compose herself. 'What are you doing here?' she muttered, her cheeks still blazing hot.

'A friend invited me.' He was gazing at her with a contemplative expression on his face now.

'What?' she asked crossly, becoming even more uncomfortable under his intense gaze.

'Nothing,' he said. 'I just wasn't expecting to see you here. Especially not so much of you,' he added, grinning at her now. 'You haven't changed since you were little, you know.'

'Is that supposed to be a compliment or an insult?'

They were interrupted by a pretty girl with long, blonde hair gliding over and, ignoring Daisy, putting a proprietorial hand on his shoulder.

Daisy was annoyed to feel a familiar stab of jealously at the sight of it, but on the other hand, also recognised it as the perfect opportunity to get away.

'Excuse me, I have to find my friend,' she blustered, pushing past him before he could reply.

Claire was deep in conversation with a tall, auburn-haired man in a corner, so Daisy quickly diverted to the bathroom and sat on the flipped down loo lid with her head in her hands, trying to straighten herself out.

'Breathe,' she whispered to herself, taking deep gulps of air into her lungs until her head stopped spinning.

How the hell did Zach get better and better looking, every time she saw him?

She was *so annoyed* by her body's customary involuntary response to him.

Memories of their last encounter swam vividly into her mind, but she pushed them out again, getting up from the loo and going to stare into the mirror.

Get it together. It's just Zach. He can't hurt you any more than he already has.

She took another deep breath, repaired her lipstick with a shaking hand – to be ready and armoured in case she had to face him again – and nodded at herself in the mirror.

Must stay calm, she told herself, although calm was the last thing she was feeling right at that moment.

As she was leaving the bathroom, heading back towards the corner where she'd last seen Claire, she bumped into a woman walking the other way and nearly sent the drink she was carrying flying.

'Sorry,' Daisy muttered, holding up her hand in apology.

'Daisy? Is that you?' said the woman.

Daisy stopped in her tracks and turned to face her.

'Carol?' Daisy was both pleased and pained to bump into her old friend right at that moment. Carol and Daisy had been at university together and even though they'd never been especially close, they'd spent a number of crazy nights out together with the same group of friends, touring the clubs and bars of Manchester.

Carol was a tiny thing with a mass of red hair and an abundance of freckles on her button nose. She reminded Daisy of a doll and had always been so full of energy, she'd made her feel tired just being around her.

'It is you!' Carol said with a huge smile. 'How are you? It's been ages. What are you up to?'

'I live here in London. I'm a radio producer. You?'

'Actress,' Carol said. 'I'm in a play on in the West End at the moment.'

'That's amazing. Well done you!'

They chatted for a bit and as Carol was frenziedly explaining what a fantastic life she was now leading, a large, male presence walking towards them caught Daisy's eye.

Zach.

Daisy braced herself for another jibe, but to her surprise, he wrapped his arms around Carol's shoulders and placed his chin on the top of her head, smiling his heart-stopping smile at Daisy.

Her heart sank.

Typical. Of course he was now seeing someone she knew and liked so she couldn't hate her for it.

Carol looked round to see who was wrapped around her and gently punched him on the arm.

'Hey, Zach, this is my friend, Daisy, from university.'

'Actually, she's my friend from a very long time ago,' he said, looking at Daisy searchingly.

She smiled weakly back at him.

The same desire to put her hands on him – all over him, in fact – was back with a vengeance. But this was the man who'd played with her emotions, refused to listen to her version of events and told her he never wanted to see her again, she reminded herself. And to top it off, he was obviously with her old uni friend now and quite prepared to lord it over her.

'Where's Adam? Is he here?' Zach asked, but was

drowned out by Carol blurting, 'We should all meet up for a drink soon then. It'd be great to catch up properly. Give me your number, Daisy.' She looked at Zach. 'Have you got your phone on you? Mine's in my coat pocket in the cloakroom.'

Daisy was glad of the interruption. He obviously hadn't heard about her and Adam then, if he was asking about him, and the last thing she wanted was for Zach to find out she was on her own now. Especially after the way things had ended with Adam. It was a matter of pride.

He hesitated for a moment, then nodded and produced his phone. 'I'm afraid I don't have your new number,' he said to Daisy.

Of course, he'd never had her number, or she his. They'd stayed in contact through Adam.

Daisy felt trapped. It would look really weird if she refused to give it. So, she dictated her phone number and Carol tapped it into Zach's phone.

'There you go.' She handed the phone back to Zach. 'Text it to me, will you?'

'Sure thing,' he agreed, glancing surreptitiously at Daisy from under his dark lashes.

She had no idea what he was thinking, or even how she was supposed to feel about all this any more.

Carol broke into her thoughts. 'Hey, Zach, I forgot to ask, did you beat Nathaniel Kingson to that part you were talking about?'

Daisy saw Zach visibly bristle at this name. She had a vague memory of hearing it before, but was struggling to remember where.

'I'm pleased to say I did.' He turned to look at her, right in the eyes. 'Sorry, Daisy,' he added with a strange hint of sarcasm. 'I know how much you admire him.'

Daisy stared back at him in confusion. She didn't even know who this guy was.

'I met him once,' continued Carol. 'He's a real sleazebag. Apparently, he tries it on with practically every woman he meets. "My friends call me Sonny, I hope you're going to be one of them",' she mimicked in a smooth, deep American voice.

This was apparently a good imitation of him, because Zach pulled a face, in what looked like disgusted recognition.

Daisy, on the other hand, had a sudden, horrible, moment of clarity.

No.

Fuck.

It couldn't have been him.

Could it?

The guy she'd met in the café in Cannes. The same guy that had rescued her after Adam had punched Zach.

The guy that Zach had seen her kissing...

Anguish flooded through her and she stared, unseeingly, at the floor as she tried to get her thoughts in order.

Zach had told her he was the guy that had slept with the casting director for the part that Zach really wanted.

He was his *nemesis*.

She almost laughed. Almost.

It really wasn't funny though.

No wonder he'd been so angry with her.

He thought she was attracted to the guy he despised most in the world.

The guy he'd opened up his heart to her about, in a very un-Zach like manner.

Hot shame trickled through her.

But it wasn't all her fault. He hadn't given her a chance to explain and had immediately accused her of being a film star groupie, proving how little he really trusted her. What had he said? 'I never thought you had stars in your eyes'. It hadn't made any sense to her at the time, but everything slotted into place now she knew which part of the puzzle it fitted into.

Her heart was racing again now and she felt a bit sick with it. She had to get out of there, away from him and back to normality, back to a place where she felt comfortable and safe. Where she could think straight.

'I've got to go,' she announced, aware of how abrupt she sounded, but not able to care right at that moment. 'Bye.'

Without looking back at them, she hurried through the club and out into the cool night air, pausing only to grab her coat from the receptionist by the door.

She was only aware that Zach had followed her when she stopped to look desperately up and down the road for any sign of a taxi.

'Daisy, wait. Please. I need to talk to you. I think I might have made a mistake,' he said, walking up to where she was standing in the middle of the street.

She was amazed to hear him say this, but could she believe he really meant it? Right at that moment, she didn't have the energy for one of their games.

I have to nip this in the bud right now. It's wrecking my head.

She spun round to face him. 'Yes, you did. So did I, trying to be friends with you. It was never going to work. Relationships are built on trust, Zach, but you didn't trust that I was a better person than that. You called me a manipulative bitch!'

He looked at her steadily for a moment, then ran a hand over his hair in apparent agitation. 'Yeah. I know. You're right. I wanted to clear the air about that.'

'Look, why don't you just get back to Carol and leave me alone,' she said forcefully, on the brink of tears now. Tears she really didn't want him to see.

'Carol? What's she got to do with this?' He looked confused.

'Don't you think she'll be upset if she finds you're out here, chasing after me?'

He frowned. 'Why would she?' Realisation suddenly seemed to dawn on him. 'We're not seeing each other. We work together. We're in a play together at the moment.'

'Oh.' She didn't know what to do now, what to think. Her composure was in pieces. She needed some space to pull herself together, so she turned and started walking quickly away from him.

He came after her, walking alongside, matching

her pace. 'Jesus. You always jump to the wrong conclusion!'

'*I* always jump to the wrong conclusion?'

'We don't seem to be able to be in each other's company without getting angry,' he said with a deep sigh.

'No, we don't. We're not good together and I can't live like that. It's too stressful. So, perhaps it's best if we stay away from each other.'

Did she really mean that?

Did she?

'Daisy, wait. Look, just stop for a minute and talk to me,' Zach said, his voice holding a conciliatory note now.

This was all too much for her right now though. It felt so hopeless. The tears were so close.

'I can't deal with this right now. I don't know how to feel about you any more. Please, just leave me alone.' Turning away from him, she picked up her pace.

She sensed him dropping back, letting her go, so she strode on purposefully towards the main road, forcing herself not to look back.

She was afraid for a minute that he'd start following her again and see the tears that were now cascading down her face, but luckily, he didn't.

Thankfully, she managed to hail a taxi on the main road and jumped in, quickly giving directions to her house before bursting into loud sobs, much to the obvious discomfort of the driver.

17

A week later, after having had no further contact from Zach, Daisy made her weary way home from work. It had been another tough day, with her trying not to think about him and break down in tears.

Clearly, he'd taken her demand for him to leave her alone seriously.

She'd dreamt about him pretty much every night since she'd last seen him, never remembering exactly what had happened in the dream when she woke up, but being left with an intense feeling of sexual longing and deep disquiet.

He was terrible for her mental health, she knew that, so why couldn't she stop yearning for him?

Her mobile started ringing as she stepped in

through the front door on Friday night and she had to rummage frantically around in her bag before locating it. She didn't recognise the number, but answered anyway, just in case it was something to do with work. Or something.

'Hi, Dizzy, it's Zach,' came a deep, breathtakingly familiar voice on the other end.

Her heart immediately began to race.

Play it cool, Daisy.

'What do you want?' she asked, trying to keep the tremor out of her voice.

'I was hoping I could see you. We need to straighten some things out.'

So many thoughts filled her head. Could she handle this conversation right now?

'Please, Diz, I know I've always acted like an idiot towards you, but you're one of my oldest friends and I'd really like to see you again. No funny business, I promise. Bring Adam with you if you want. If he'll deign to come,' he added.

Daisy sighed.

Tell him, a voice in her head urged her. There really wasn't any point dodging the issue any longer; he was bound to find out from someone else soon.

'I'm not with Adam any more. We split up.'

There was a long silence at the other end of the phone.

'What?' Zach said eventually, his voice gruff and surprisingly shaky sounding. 'What happened?'

'Nothing, we just grew apart. It had nothing to do with you,' she added quickly.

Liar.

'I don't believe you, Daisy,' he said quietly, as if reading her thoughts. 'Are you still in the same flat?'

'Yes, but—' she started to say, but Zach interrupted with a curt, 'I'm coming over.'

'Wait... Zach—' but he'd already put the phone down.

So, all she could do now was mark time until he arrived.

Every nerve in her body jangled.

She was a mess.

Definitely not in any fit state to see Zach right now.

She'd been working in a hot studio all day and looked like hell.

She ran upstairs and quickly took a shower, then dressed with shaking hands.

She checked, then double checked her appearance, brushed her teeth, sprayed herself with perfume and changed her clothes again.

It was imperative she felt completely in control when he arrived.

After pacing up and down her living room for a few minutes, she heard a loud banging on the door. Taking a deep breath, she opened it.

Zach stood there on her doorstep, gazing at her.

He looked so good, it took her breath away.

'Why didn't you tell me before?' he demanded, in his customary gruff manner.

'I... I don't know. I guess I was afraid.'

'Of what?'

'Of what you might do. Or what *I* might do.'

Zach walked inside, closing the door behind him and, taking her gently by the arm, he marched her into the living room and guided her down onto the sofa.

He sat down next to her and took hold of her hands, gripping them tightly so she couldn't get away.

Not that she found she wanted to.

'What are you doing?' she asked, staring down at their locked fingers, her voice coming out all breathy.

'I want you to stay still till I've had a chance to say what needs to be said,' he replied.

She could feel him looking at her and he waited till she looked right back at him.

'Daisy, I'm in love with you. I always have been. We're meant to be together.'

Heat rushed to her cheeks. Could he be serious, this emotionally closed, angry man?

But then *was* he that any more?

'Please believe me, Diz,' he said. 'Say you love me back. I know you do.'

Should she say it? It was true, she *did* love him and always would, that was perfectly plain to her now. But she was terrified this wasn't real. What if it was just another one of his games? One he was determined to win. It had always been a battle of wills between them and this was no exception.

'Nah,' she whispered, staring defiantly back at him.

His eyes flashed with frustration, but also with challenge.

'You're a liar,' he growled. 'I'm going to get you to say it.'

Before she knew what was happening, he leaned forwards and pressed his mouth against hers, urging her lips to part so his tongue could slide against hers.

A wave of desire washed through her from head

to toe and she moaned, deep in her throat, despite her intention to stand up to him.

After a moment of sweet torture, he pulled away from the kiss, leaving both of them panting for air. 'Say it, Diz.'

'I don't think I will,' she said, though failing to say it with as much conviction this time.

Raising an eyebrow, he let go of her hands and slid one of his own against her jaw, drawing her gently, but intently towards him again, so their lips were nearly touching.

His breath stroked her skin as he hovered there, his mouth millimetres away from hers.

'Say it,' he whispered against her lips, his intense gaze locked with hers.

'Uh-uh,' she whispered back.

To her consternation, he pulled suddenly away from her and she almost gave him the *yes* he was so desperate to hear, until he smiled his devastating smile and reached forwards and started to tug at the buttons of her blouse, sliding them out of the material, one by one, until the whole thing gaped open, revealing her lacy bra.

The game was still very much on.

Putting his hands on her shoulders – and keeping his gaze locked with hers the whole time –

he pushed the blouse down her arms, trapping them against her body, then did the same with her bra straps.

She drew in a ragged breath, but didn't fight or help him in any way.

He was carefully checking her face now, to make sure she was actually okay with this and she guessed it must have reflected her need for him to continue because a moment later, he pulled down the cups of her bra too, then bent towards her, lowering his head so his lips could graze first one nipple, then the other, sending waves of excitement through her body.

She moaned again at the intensity of the feeling.

The wonderful scent and the heat of him were making her feel dizzy and a familiar, low throb had begun deep in the heart of her. She could feel how wet she was already between her thighs, in anticipation of what she was sure was about to happen. What she hoped would happen.

And she was going to let it.

But not just yet.

Because she knew she had the power here – even though they were both pretending that wasn't the case.

She trusted he would stop if she asked him to.

'Say it,' he murmured, starting to move further down her body, placing hard kisses against her ribs, her stomach, her hipbones...

'Nope,' she whispered, not meaning it one bit now, her breath coming in short gasps.

She'd never felt such elation and was revelling in the pretend struggle she was putting up, teasing him, forcing him to take more and more drastic action.

His hands grasped the hem of her skirt, which he slid up her legs to expose her knickers to him.

Slipping his fingers into the top band of them, he pushed the flimsy material down her legs until she was completely exposed to his gaze and lowered his mouth to her there, sweeping her clitoris with his tongue in a long, firm stroke.

The intensity of feeling made her shout out and she arched her body closer to him, desperate to feel his touch there again.

He began to stroke her rhythmically with his tongue, sending spasms of pleasure through her body. She'd never felt these sensations so intensely before and she could quite happily have let it go on forever.

As if sensing this, he lifted his head and looked at her, breaking the exquisite contact.

'Say it, Diz,' he said quietly.

Daisy stared into his beautiful face.

'Don't stop,' she pleaded.

A look of triumph came over his face.

'I want to make love to you. Let me? Please?' he implored, his pupils dilated with lust.

Daisy nodded. 'Do it.'

Zach stood up and quickly pulled off his shirt, then tugged at his belt, looking down at Daisy the whole time. He still had a wonderfully toned, sleek body, just as she remembered him.

Stepping out of his trousers and boxers, he left them in a heap on the floor and inserted his legs between her spread thighs.

She lay there, gazing up at him from the sofa in wonder, her whole body feeling like it was on fire with the need for him to be inside her.

Lowering himself, so his body pressed firmly against hers, he returned his mouth to hers, kissing her urgently now.

She gasped as he entered her, waves of the most exquisite pleasure rushing through her as they began to move together.

'Oh, God,' Zach groaned. 'Daisy, I love you. I love you.'

It felt so good to have him inside her again.

So *right*.

They fit perfectly together, like their bodies were made for each other.

He leaned in closer to her so his pelvis brushed against hers rhythmically, again and again until she felt waves of the most intense orgasm she'd ever experienced ripple through her, sending a rushing sensation through her head, blood pounding in her ears, her body overwhelmed with pleasure.

He came moments later, thrusting hard into her.

They lay pressed together, their chests heaving and their limbs wrapped tightly around each other.

Sated and elated.

When they'd both caught their breath, Zach gently rolled off her and after helping her properly remove the rest of her clothes, pulled her close against his body again, kissing her face and hair.

'Are you okay?' he asked quietly.

She looked at him and smiled. 'Yes.'

His brow pinched into a frown as he stroked the hair away from her face. 'I know I've made a god-awful mess of everything up till now and I'm really sorry. I've been so jealous of Adam. I wanted you so much, but I didn't know what to do to prove that I loved you. You always seemed angry with me, no matter how many times I tried to apologise.' He sighed and ran a hand over his own tousled hair.

Daisy was lost for words. He was right. She'd been really afraid to trust him, but she truly believed now, deep down, that he did love her. 'I'm sorry too. I was scared that you were just playing games with me,' she whispered. 'But I know you weren't.'

He drew his head back to look into her eyes. 'Please say it now, Daisy.'

'Okay.' She cupped his jaw and looked right back at him. 'I'm in love with you and I always will be.'

He finally smiled, the expression on his face the happiest she'd ever seen him.

* * *

They lay in each other's arms for a long while, enjoying the closeness of their bodies as they gently dozed.

After a while, Zach turned to kiss along her shoulder to her throat, then up to her mouth. After teasing her with his tongue and biting down gently on her bottom lip, he pulled away and gazed at her.

'You're so gorgeous. I've never met anyone who can equal you in beauty,' he said, kissing her again.

She pulled away from him with one ironic eyebrow raised. 'What, not even all those glamorous women you've dated?' she asked, not daring to believe the compliment but desperately hoping to be contradicted.

'You're kidding me. Most of them have turned out to be self-centred attention seekers. I felt like I was playing a part the whole time I was in a relationship with any of them. You met Lola, right? I only had to mention that we were close once and she turned into this crazy-jealous person I didn't recognise,' he said, grimacing as if reliving it in his mind. 'But you... you're the real deal. You know me better than anyone. By which I mean you know what an irascible bastard I am, but you love me anyway. I need you, Daisy, to save me from myself,' he said with a teasing grin. 'You're so genuine. No pretentions. That's what makes you so beautiful: that and your amazing eyes,' he added. 'Even when we were children, you just blew me away. When I first saw you again at the anniversary party in Fowey, I thought my heart was going to stop.'

Daisy looked at him in surprise.

'Really? I had no idea you felt like that. I guess I was too concerned about how you were making *me* feel. I dropped that glass bowl of fruit salad all over the floor at the sight of you.'

Zach laughed, his dark eyes twinkling. 'I just put that down to your usual clumsiness,' he teased.

She slapped his arm playfully. 'No, not that time, at least.'

He propped his head on his hand. 'Did you really find me attractive then? I had no idea. You seemed much more interested in Adam.'

Daisy grimaced. 'I was confused about how I felt about you. I thought you weren't interested in me and Adam came along professing his love and I didn't know what to do.'

She glanced at him. His face was set in a frown.

'Don't be cross. I was so young and naïve; I didn't think I could handle you. You seemed so self-assured and...' she paused trying to find the right words, '... so hard.'

He glanced away from her when she said that. His face tense and troubled. 'I know.' He sighed and rubbed at his eyes. 'I wasn't in a good mental place when I was young. Well, you know all about my upbringing. I *was* hard. I didn't really feel any love from my dad. That's why I care about the Carmichaels so much. They saved me from going completely off the rails.'

'Yeah, they're really good people. That's why I love them too. I feel like they'd always have my back if I needed them to.'

Zach nodded in agreement. 'Yeah.' He paused for

a moment, then took a breath before he spoke again, as if he wasn't sure about the wisdom of saying the next thing.

'You know, Sally kind of warned me off you when we were younger. Not that she was really blatant about it. She just suggested I give you some space. I think she thought I was too angry for you. I guess she wasn't wrong. Trouble was, it only made me want you more. I really hated being told what to do – or what not to do – when I was young. Still do.' He gave her a rueful grin.

'No kidding,' she agreed, grinning back.

'But I love her like she's my own mother so I tried to do what she asked. But it was so fucking hard, Daisy. I had no idea how to be friends with you. I always wanted more than that. So I was really con-fused about how to act around you when we were young. And then when we got locked in that cellar. *Jesus.* The way you looked at me: with such defi-ance... and such heat. You always knew exactly how to push my buttons.'

He reached out and stroked her face.

'I totally went to pieces. Before and after. I felt so shitty about going against her wishes, but I *really* fucking wanted you. I wanted *you* to be my first. I'm sorry I made you believe otherwise. I was really cruel to you, but I swear I was trying to protect you, and myself of course. I've always been a self-serving arsehole. Still am.'

Pulling him to her, she hugged him hard. 'I guess you've had to be because of the way you were forced to grow up,' she whispered into his neck.

He pulled away from her and lay back on the cushion, staring up at the ceiling. 'Yeah. Probably. Not that that's a good excuse for how I treated you. And Adam too. I don't think Sally knew how Adam felt about you at that point, but I did. It was so obvious in the way he talked about you – which was all the bloody time – and the way his behaviour changed when he was around you. He never said anything directly to me, but he didn't need to. There was this unspoken agreement between us. He was my best friend. If he hadn't been, God knows what would have happened to me. He was my family. Him, Sally, Andy and Sam. And the last thing I wanted to do was fuck that up. I loved them all. Still do. Unfortunately, you got caught up in it all. Not that I regret what we did. Not for a second.'

He turned to look at her again now. 'Having sex with you was the most meaningful experience of my life. And I very much want to keep doing it. If you'll let me?'

He lifted his hand to stroke his fingers down her throat, then down to her breasts, where he circled his fingertip around her nipple.

She shivered with pleasure. 'Fine by me.'

'I've always felt this intense need to protect you,' he murmured. 'I wanted to keep you safe. Perhaps because I didn't feel safe myself and I was projecting? That's what my counsellor thinks, anyway.'

'Makes sense,' she said, finding it increasingly difficult to concentrate on replying as his fingertips moved down over her stomach, and lower.

'I knew from an early age I was completely in love with you, but I was afraid you'd reject me if I told you how I felt. I just wasn't brave enough to go after you myself and I missed my chance.'

'How early an age?' she managed to struggle out, as his fingertips slid over her mound and into the damp, waiting heat between her legs.

'Since I first met you, I think, so twelve? Though if I had to put an exact time on when I knew it for sure, it'd be when you broke that bone in your foot and I could see how scared and in pain you were, but you were trying so hard to hide it from me. You were always so brave. I think I fell totally in love with you at that moment.'

Daisy was astounded by this confession. She'd

had no idea he'd felt all this, and from such a young age too. She was suddenly, desperately sad for the lost, lonely boy he used to be.

She reached down and stilled his hand, holding it against her body, but needing to pause the riot of sensations he was drawing from her so she could concentrate fully on what he was saying.

Zach looked at her, his eyes searching hers, clearly wondering whether he was freaking her out by admitting all this.

'You can see why I acted the way I did, can't you?' he said. 'I'm not trying to excuse any of it, I know it was shitty behaviour and I said and did some bloody awful things, but I loved you so much, I couldn't bear the thought of never being part of your life. It made me crazy.'

'It's okay,' she said, 'I get it.' She drew his head towards her and kissed him hard. 'You're right. We're meant to be together; I've always felt that too. Always just known it. Deep down.'

She rolled on top of him, straddling him and lining herself up with his body, then slowly lowered herself down onto his rock-hard erection, taking him deep inside her.

He let out a loud, deep groan as she began to move above him.

Putting his hands on her hips, he helped her move so they were perfectly in sync with each other, her pressing down and him thrusting up at the same time.

It was utter bliss.

She came first and he followed her not long afterwards, his fingers digging hard into her hips.

Smiling to herself, she dropped her mouth to his and kissed him deeply, drinking in the delicious scent and taste of him, her heart fluttering in her chest.

He was all hers now.

* * *

They finally dragged themselves out of bed – or rather, off the sofa – and went in search of food. Daisy hadn't been shopping recently so they snacked on oat cakes, cheese and fruit, which suited Daisy fine as she was having trouble locating her hunger.

They sat in companionable silence while they ate.

After finishing her food, Daisy glanced over at Zach as he poured himself a glass of wine from a bottle which she'd fortuitously unearthed from the back of a cupboard.

He obviously felt her watching him because he looked up and gave her a questioning look.

'Why did you invite Adam and me to Cannes?'

He paused for a moment, seeming to consider his answer. 'Partly because I missed you both and wanted to see you, partly to show off how amazingly well I was doing – to try and temper my jealousy about the two of you being together, but I also badly wanted to make it up to you, for my awful behaviour when I came to stay with Lola,' he said, pausing to take a sip of his wine. 'I told myself I had to get used to the idea of you and Adam being together because I really couldn't stand the thought of losing your friendships. I don't have anyone else in this world that I love the way I love you two. You and the Carmichaels are my only *real* friends.'

He looked at her slightly shamefully. 'And I suppose, deep down, I always hoped you and Adam would have an amicable split and I'd be around to help you pick up the pieces. Maybe on that trip? I don't know. I was so caught up with how much I missed you, I wasn't really thinking straight.' He frowned down at the table. 'I also didn't properly consider how all this would affect Adam.'

Daisy leaned over the table and cupped his face

with her hands, turning it gently so he was looking at her.

'Don't beat yourself up about it. It wasn't just your fault, it was mine too and Adam's, to some extent. We each wanted something from the other, but were too blind to see the best thing for us all at the time.'

Zach nodded and smiled and she released his jaw and sat back down in her chair, hopeful he'd accepted her point.

'How is Adam?' he asked tentatively.

'I don't know to be perfectly honest. After he left, I didn't hear from him again. He's found someone else to love though, so at least he isn't on his own. She's called Suzie, apparently, and he'd been sleeping with her before we split up.'

'Really?' Zach was surprised. 'Fast work, Adam – and a little underhand, considering the shit he's given us when we've never really done anything physical behind his back.'

'Hmm, I'm not entirely sure we can claim that,' she said, with a rueful grin. 'And we've been having an emotional affair with each other for years.'

Zach nodded slowly. 'Yeah, I guess you're right. We're all as bad as each other. We've really tangled ourselves into knots here.'

'He and I had been pretty rocky for some time, anyway,' Daisy admitted. 'We'd slowly grown apart, so there was a lot of time for us both to get used to the idea we weren't going to be together forever.' She felt a wash of sadness at this confession, but it was true. Deep down, she truly believed they'd both known they wouldn't last.

'Do you think he'll ever forgive us?' Zach asked.

'I don't know. I hope so. Maybe in time.' Despite everything, she couldn't bear the thought of never seeing Adam again. He'd been part of her life for as long as she could remember and the thought of never speaking to him again was devastating.

Zach obviously felt the same, judging by the expression on his face.

After a minute's contemplation, he waved a hand at her. 'Don't worry. I'll explain it all to him. Talk to him properly about it all for once. Finally be straight about how I feel. Hopefully, he'll do the same. I'll get through to him eventually,' Zach said. 'I know him. He won't stay mad at us forever. It may take time and a lot of effort on our part, but he'll come around, especially if he's really in love with this Suzie now. You wait and see.'

Daisy felt relief sweep through her. If anyone could reach Adam, it would be Zach. There was too much history between them for Adam to just give up on them. She snuggled in close to him. Just the scent of him made her feel euphoric. Could she really, finally be here, in his arms? She'd always felt, deep down, that it might happen, but she'd never dared to hope.

Something was still troubling her, though.

'Zach...' she said tentatively.

'Yes, Daisy,' he said, looking at her from under his long, dark lashes.

'About what happened on the boat. With Nathaniel.'

Zach tensed at the sound of his name, but she carried on regardless. This needed to be sorted out, once and for all.

'I really didn't know who he was, you know.'

He just looked at her, waiting for further explanation.

'I met him in a café the day of the party. I had no idea he was even an actor. He introduced himself to me as Sonny in exactly the way Carol said he does to every woman he meets.' She blushed at the memory of the shame she'd felt when she finally realised who he was.

'Yeah. Nathaniel Kingson. Apparently, the cheesy fucker calls himself 'Sonny' to women, which he pretends is a nickname his friends gave him, but word has it he made it up himself.'

She made a face of disgust. 'After Adam hit you, I was mortified. I felt like everyone at the party was laughing and pointing at me. Nathaniel came over and "rescued me". I thought he was being kind and I got a bit swept up in the moment. I never intended to kiss him. He just sort of leant into me and it took me a moment to realise what was happening. I was so mixed up about how I felt about you and about Adam, I just let him do it. I'm so sorry, I know what it must have looked like, but please believe me, it meant absolutely nothing to me.'

She waited, her confession hanging in the air between them.

'But you told me you knew who he was,' Zach said gruffly, after a moment, confusion written all over his face. 'Remember? That night we went out for a meal, before we went to the casino.'

Daisy was baffled. She desperately searched her memory for the conversation. Then it hit her. When Zach had told her about how Nathaniel had won that part that he'd wanted she'd tried to be kind and make him feel better by pretending to know who he was, but not to think much of him.

'Ah,' she said. 'Well, the thing is… I lied.'

Zach just looked at her, eyebrows raised.

'I only said I knew who he was because I wanted to make you feel better about yourself.'

'You pitied me.' This, he said as a statement and Daisy was afraid for a moment that she'd mortally offended him.

'No, of course not,' she said quickly. 'I was having so much fun with you that night and you were so open with me. It was the first time you'd ever let me into your head. I just wanted to let you know that I cared about you and hated anyone who wanted to hurt you.'

There was a silence.

'Zach? Please believe me.'

'I do,' he said, his expression softening.

Daisy was so relieved she leant across the table and hugged him to her.

'I truly had no idea who he really was that night. I never meant to kiss him. I wouldn't knowingly do that to you.' She said this against his hair, breathing in its delicious, musky scent.

'I know. I asked him about it,' Zach said, pulling gently away from the embrace.

She sat back down with a thump in her chair. 'You asked him?'

'Yeah, I had to know what had actually happened, so I just asked him outright when I next saw him. He said he'd rescued you and just thought he'd have a go. "Nothing to lose", as he put it. Prick. You did look particularly beautiful that night, so I can't really blame him.'

Daisy felt a familiar warmth rush to her face.

Zach crossed his arms, his shoulders a little tense now. 'He said he didn't know you were my girlfriend and I had to admit that you weren't. That cut me to the core. He's such a smug bastard and made it perfectly clear he thought I was a real loser to have missed my chance with you.' He snorted. 'For once, I agreed with him.'

He leaned over and gently brushed his thumb against her cheek, sending shivers through all her nerve endings.

'I *was* an idiot. After that night in Monte Carlo... I'd started to hope there might be something between us. That you didn't find me completely untrustworthy. I told myself I'd leave it up to you to decide about us, but of course my natural instinct was to keep pushing you until you realised I was the one you should be with. Then, when I saw you,' he paused, a frown creasing his face again now, 'kissing Kingson,' he looked her directly in the eyes. 'I thought my heart was going to break.' His gaze darted away as colour rose in his cheeks. 'Now who's the cheesy fucker.'

At this admission, Daisy felt her eyes well with tears and she hurriedly brushed them away as they started to trickle down her face.

'Daisy, don't cry. I'm so sorry. The last thing I wanted was to hurt you.' He splayed his hands on the table and stared down at them. 'You're the only woman I've ever loved – apart from Sally, but that's more of a maternal thing.'

Daisy nodded, smiling through her tears, unable to speak for fear of breaking down.

She was terrified she'd lose it completely and start bawling, just to release all the pent-up pain and hurt she'd been carrying around for such a long time now.

'Daisy...' Zach said, gently touching her arm, 'I don't know how to make it up to you. If you need to scream at me, do it. It's okay. I deserve it.'

Just hearing him say this deflated the tension in her and she shook her head again, pausing for a moment to collect herself.

'I'm not angry with you. I never was. It was the situation we were in that's caused so many problems, and so much heartache. Poor Adam. I never should have let our relationship carry on when I knew that it was *you* I was in love with.'

At this, Zach stood up and moved round the table, lifting her out of her seat and crushing her against him in a fierce hug.

'Oh, my God, Daisy. We wasted so much time,' he whispered into her hair.

She pulled back from him and looked deep into his eyes. His pupils were so dilated, they seemed almost entirely black.

'Then let's not waste any more,' she suggested, kissing his mouth, which curled into a huge smile, before he kissed her back.

Before she knew what was happening, he carried her into the bedroom and lay her down on the bed. Without speaking, he methodically stripped first her clothes off her, then his own off him, before joining her on the mattress.

When he slipped his hand between her legs, she knew he'd find how ready for him she already was. So, without preamble this time, he slid inside her, smiling as she let out a low moan of pleasure.

'Oh my God, that feels so good,' she murmured.

He began to move, drawing long strokes in and out of her, then pausing before he pushed himself back deep inside her, till she thought she'd go crazy with it.

Deciding to teach him a lesson for teasing her, she clenched around the length of him, as hard as she could, whilst raising her pelvis and urging his thrusts to go deeper.

Zach groaned at the added pressure, his breath coming fast and heavy now.

'Wait, Daisy, wait... I don't I want to come yet,' he muttered.

But it was too late. He tipped over the edge, his body shuddering hard as he came inside her, a low growl escaping from his throat.

They lay there, panting for a moment, limbs wrapped tightly around each other.

'Hmm, a reluctant orgasm. That's really hot,' she said finally, with a grin.

She felt him laugh into her hair.

Drawing himself out of her, he slid his hand back between her legs and used his fingers to make her come too, kissing her hard as she climaxed and trapping her cry of release in his mouth.

After an age, they untangled themselves and looked at each other, their soft breathing the only sound in the room.

Zach seemed to hesitate for a moment before

saying, 'I should probably wait and make some big expensive gesture before doing this, but I just can't. I've waited too long already. Will you marry me?'

She gasped, feeling her world falling perfectly into place for the very first time.

'Yes, yes, yes!' she said, overcome with a feeling of exquisite rightness.

They held each other tightly, rocking from side to side, laughing and hugging.

'So,' Zach said finally, 'what do we do to celebrate?' He grinned at her, wickedly.

'I'm sure we can think of something,' Daisy replied, waggling her eyebrows, a slow smile stealing over her face, as she pulled him towards her again for a long, loving kiss.

EPILOGUE

SIX YEARS LATER

The air was still and clement in the quaint, Cornish, seaside town of Fowey, where two families were staying for a well-deserved summer holiday.

The sun danced on the waves in the distance and its lingering rays caused the gently swaying trees in their garden to cast long shadows across the lawn of the grand, Edwardian house.

Three young children raced around the garden, enjoying the last of the day's warmth, completely unaware of the adults in the living room looking out at them.

Zach strolled into the room and wrapped his arms around his wife, nuzzling into her neck and sending shivers of pleasure down her spine. Even after all this time, he could still turn her to jelly just by touching her.

Daisy craned her neck to look up at him and smiled.

'Where have you been?' she asked. He smelled of fresh air and salt.

'Just went for a quick stroll down to the beach to clear my head,' he replied, kissing her gently on the lips.

'All right, you two,' came a deep voice from the corner of the room. 'We don't need to be subjected to your public displays of affection every minute of the day, thanks very much.' This was said with humour, though there was a mocking dryness to Adam's tone.

They both rolled their eyes at him. He was one to talk. He could barely keep his hands off Suzie whenever she was within ten feet of him.

Adam stood up and stretched his arms above his head. 'I suppose we should get them to come in for some tea,' he said, nodding towards the garden where the children were happily playing.

'Ah, leave them for a bit longer,' Suzie said, coming into the room with a tray of pre-dinner drinks.

Once the strangeness of meeting Adam's new partner had worn off, Daisy had found she really

liked Suzie. She was such a positive person and perfectly suited to him.

Not for the first time, Daisy felt a warm sense of
satisfaction at the way things had turned out.

It had taken Zach a while to persuade Adam to
give him a hearing, but he'd been determined to do
it. He'd spent months wearing him down. He'd call
or drop in on him at regular intervals, until his old
friend was forced to hear what he had to say, just to
get rid of him. They'd argued a lot and many a time,
Zach had come home to Daisy frustrated and angry
at his inability to breach the gap that had grown between them all.

Adam had a huge amount of resentment built up
and wasn't willing to let them back into his good
books in a hurry. He had, after all, been subjected to
years of angst and jealousy when it came to the relationship between Zach and Daisy and was unwilling
to get himself back involved with them in case it
brought all the old feelings and paranoia back.

He was well supported by Suzie, who approved
of his rejection of Zach at first, but who came to see
how much Adam was affected by the loss of his
friendship with his two oldest and closest friends.

It was her that had finally persuaded him to

listen to what Zach had to say and begin the long, hard road to forgiveness.

He'd chipped away at him slowly, gently offering sincere regrets, until Adam's attitude began to soften.

Finally, he admitted to Zach that he could see how right he and Daisy were for each other and that his years of loving them from the time they were children was just too strong to ignore.

Then, when three years ago, Daisy had fallen pregnant with their son, Max, and Suzie had also found herself pregnant with her and Adam's daughter, Rosie, they'd all become good friends again, even going so far as to take holidays together.

Daisy gazed at their children, chasing each other around the trees. Her son and Adam's daughter were as thick as thieves, being a very similar age, and her younger daughter, Felicity, who had come along just a year after Max, was desperately trying to break into the close friendship that had formed between the older children.

'Look well if those two end up getting together when they're older,' Zach murmured into her ear. She chuckled at the thought. 'I wouldn't mind, as long as they don't have to go through all the angst that we did,' she said.

* * *

Later that evening, all the adults went out for a meal to a local restaurant, leaving the children in the capable hands of a babysitter they'd found through a well-reputed agency.

Zach still drew excited looks from other restaurant-goers whenever they went out, but the attention was now less fierce since he'd stopped appearing in Hollywood films and had opted instead to take roles mostly in plays running in the UK, as well as the odd UK-set movie or show. He was happier now than he'd ever been, he told Daisy on a regular basis. He'd always wanted his own family – had been desperate for it since he was young – and the comfort it brought him now was like a dream come true.

The place they'd chosen to eat in was rowdy, but the atmosphere was friendly and they all soon settled in and ordered their food and drinks.

As soon as the waitress moved away, a young, bright-eyed woman approached their table, her gaze firmly trained on Zach.

'Excuse me, Zach?' she said, with a tremble in her voice.

Zach turned to look at her.

'Sorry to ask while you're out with friends, but

could I have a selfie with you? It would mean so much to me. I'm a huge fan. I've seen all your films.'

'Sure,' Zach said, magnanimously, even though Daisy could see he was a little uncomfortable to be singled out like this in front of Adam and Suzie.

'Thanks!' the woman said, holding out her phone in front of them and scooching down so her head was next to his. She took quite a few photos, obviously determined to walk away with at least one useable one.

'When's the next film coming out?' she asked excitedly.

'Ah. I'm taking a break from films. My wife's not keen on me swanning off to the States all the time.' He nudged Daisy gently, flashing her a teasing grin.

'Oh. What a shame,' the fan said, her face dropping.

Daisy wasn't sure whether this was from the lack of new Zach-fronted films or the fact he'd told her he was married.

'But you're not giving up acting altogether? Please tell me you're not!'

'No. No. I've got a play touring in a few months.'

The woman beamed at him. 'That's great. I can't believe I've met you here! I hope you don't mind me saying, but you're just as gorgeous in real life,' she added, her cheeks colouring.

'Thanks,' Zach said, a little stiffly.

Daisy had to stifle a giggle and when she looked over at Adam and Suzie, they seemed to be trying to squash their grins too.

'So great to meet you,' the woman said, backing away now and nearly falling over a table behind her.

As soon as she'd gone, the three of them finally let out chortles at his obvious discomfort.

'What! I have to be nice to the fans. They effectively pay my wages.' He looked cross now, but Daisy knew he wasn't really. He loved the adoration. In small doses, at least.

She was only too aware of how much he'd given up for her to keep his career based in the UK too. She *had* been uncomfortable about him travelling to the States all the time, especially when the children had come along – what with all the social media nonsense that came with it.

She'd attended red carpet events with him if he'd asked her to, but he'd always been swamped with interviews and work obligations when they were there, so it ended up not being a lot of fun after a while. He soon realised how much she disliked them and took the decision to change the trajectory his career was taking. He did a lot of voiceover work now too, which his gloriously gravelly voice suited so well, and, even better, he was able to do it from a small studio they'd set up at home.

They were still living in London but had moved to Richmond, eschewing the showiness of Primrose Hill where a number of Zach's contemporaries seemed to have settled for the lovely river walks and quiet domesticity of the pretty town.

* * *

It was pitch black when they left the restaurant and Daisy pulled her jacket around her shoulders for warmth. Even though it had been balmy earlier, the temperature had dropped with the disappearance of the sun.

Zach put his arm around her and gently drew her away from the others.

'We'll see you back at the house in a bit,' he called to Adam and Suzie as they started to head back to the holiday house.

They waved their hands in understanding and continued along the narrow road away from them.

'Where are we going?' asked Daisy, intrigued.

'You'll see,' Zach said, with an enigmatic grin.

He led her down a shallow slope and towards the sea front. They walked in silence for a minute, taking in the gentle lapping of the sea against the beach and the dark night sky with its myriad of stars twinkling overhead.

Reaching the end of a short gangplank that led them down onto the beach, they gingerly stepped their way across the sand.

They found themselves in a small cove, with steep cliffs rising majestically ahead of them, the dwindling lights of the Cornish town where they were staying glinting in the distance. Zach took her hand and lead her to a small formation of rocks, near to where the cliff started to rise out of the sand, and motioned for her to sit down.

'I found this place earlier on my walk. It's so peaceful,' he said, looking at her with love in his eyes.

'Gorgeous,' she breathed, feeling a little light headed under his adoring gaze.

What was going on here?

'I have something for you,' he said, pulling a small, black case out of his pocket.

Daisy suddenly had a strong sense of déjà vu.

Zach opened the lid of the box and offered it to her.

She gazed at the contents.

Her platinum friendship knot shone back at her, the diamond in the heart of it sparkling in the pale moonlight.

'How—?' she began, amazed at the sight of the beautiful piece of jewellery that she thought she'd lost forever. She'd admonished herself so many times since for her hasty actions on that dreadful night in Cannes all those years ago.

'I had it commissioned a few months ago, from a design I drew,' Zach said, lifting it gently out of the box and undoing the delicate clasp.

'Oh! I thought this was the one I l-lost,' Daisy stuttered in amazement.

'No. That one's still at the bottom of the Mediterranean, as far as I know,' Zach said, with one eyebrow raised in mock disapproval.

'So, that one...' she started, beginning to realise the full extent of what she had done.

'Yes, I designed that one and had it especially made too. It's one of a kind. Well, two of a kind now,' he said, putting his arms around her neck and gently fastening the clasp.

Drawing back to look at her, he gave her an admiring nod. 'Beautiful,' he said, looking straight into her eyes now.

'Oh, Zach, I'm so sorry,' she said, devastated by the thought of her previous hurtful impulsivity.

He'd had that beautiful necklace made especially for her – had taken the time to design it himself – and she'd tossed it into the sea. No wonder he'd looked so horrified when she did it. She'd thought he'd just bought it at a jeweller's shop – an expensive one, obviously – but now she realised it had meant so much more to him.

'I have a confession to make,' he said. 'It's not a friendship knot.' He looked at her steadily. 'It's a love knot. It always was, I just couldn't tell you that.'

Looking into his dark eyes, she saw a flash of the old pain that used to be there.

'I needed to be able to think of you wearing something of mine, even under false pretences, that told you how much I loved you.' He smiled sadly at the bittersweet memory. 'I'm sorry I lied to you. I promise I won't ever do it again.'

'You have nothing to be sorry for,' she said, flinging herself into his arms and kissing him passionately.

Drawing away from him, she now saw that his eyes were suffused with happiness.

'I love it. And I love you. Thank you,' she whispered, kissing him again.

'I love you too,' he murmured against her mouth. 'Just do me one favour?'

'Yes?'

'No matter how mad at me you get in the future, please don't throw this one away?' His eyes twinkled with mirth.

Daisy grinned back, kissing him hard on the mouth to seal the deal.

'I promise.'

She laughed as he picked her up in his arms and swung her round, then placed her carefully back down on the sand, so he could dance across the beach with her, the two of them moving together to their own secret rhythm.

ACKNOWLEDGEMENTS

My utmost thanks go to my brilliant editor, Megan. These characters have been in my thoughts for a long time and I'm so grateful for her encouragement and guidance in helping me bring them to shining life.

Thanks also to my wonderful friends and family. I couldn't have got through the last couple of years without you.

And finally, to you, the reader. Your support, in reading my stories, means everything.

ABOUT THE AUTHOR

Christy McKellen Formerly a Video and Radio Producer, Christy McKellen now spends her time writing romance. Over half a million copies of her books have been sold and her works have been translated into twelve different languages. She lives in the South West of England with her family.

Sign up to Christy McKellen's mailing list for news, competitions and updates on future books.

Visit Christy's website: www.christymckellen.com

Follow Christy's on social media here:

f facebook.com/christymckellenauthor
X x.com/ChristyMcKellen
O instagram.com/christymckellen
BB bookbub.com/authors/christy-mckellen

LOVE NOTES

LOVE IN EVERY CHAPTER

WHERE ALL YOUR ROMANCE
DREAMS COME TRUE!

THE HOME OF BESTSELLING
ROMANCE AND WOMEN'S
FICTION

 WARNING:
MAY CONTAIN SPICE

SIGN UP TO OUR
NEWSLETTER

https://bit.ly/Lovenotesnews

Boldw‍ood

www.ingramcontent.com/pod-product-compliance
Lightning Source LLC
Chambersburg PA
CBHW010702100726
47900CB00010B/2756